Infatuation i

and Shannon a͟r͟e s͟i͟z͟z͟l͟i͟n͟g t͟o͟g͟e͟t͟h͟e͟r i͟n a͟n͟d o͟u͟t o͟f b͟e͟d.
Miranda, Joyfully Reviewed

This story is a balance of fun, flirty and panty melting
sexiness…
Kati R, Romancing Rakes

…combines heat and emotions with humor, great
characters and fabulous dialogues, making this book fast-
paced and character-driven.
Pearl's World of Romance

It is burning up the sheets HOT!
Leagh, Romance Book Craze

This story had me enthralled from beginning to end. With
sexy yet angst-ridden men and a strong and likable
heroine, I was drawn into this world that Ms. Schroeder
created.
Words of Wisdom, A Rating

I loved this book. If you like a quick short story that pays
tribute to one of our soldiers and gives them a HEA then
you will love this book.
Book Reading Gals, A Rating

A great array of supporting characters, which I hope to see
more of in the upcoming books, smoking hot scenes ,
passion, heartfelt moments and overall a recommended
read for all !!
Page Flipperz, 4 Stars

To prove her love and save her man, she has to go above and beyond the call of duty.

Infatuation: A Little Military Harmless Romance #1

Francis McKade is a man in lust. He's had a crush on his best friend's little sister for years but he has never acted on it. Besides that fact that she's Malachi's sister, he's a Seal and he learned his lesson with his ex-fiancé. Still, at a wedding in Hawaii anything can happen—and does. Unfortunately, after the best night of his life, he's called back to duty.

Shannon is blown over by Kade. The crush she has is now developing into love. But, after months of silence, Kade walks into her bar and she gets the shock of her life. Kade isn't the man Shannon knew in Hawaii, or even the last few years. Worse, he is realizing that the career he loves just might be over.

When he pushes her to her limit in the bedroom, Shannon refuses to back down. One way or another, this military man is going to learn there is no walking away from love—not while she still has breath in her body.

Warning: This book contains two infatuated lovers, a hardheaded military man, a determined woman, some old friends, and a little taste of New Orleans. As always, ice water is suggested while reading. It might be the first military Harmless book, but the only thing that has changed is how hot our hero looks in his uniform—not to mention out of it.

Dedication

To the men and women of the United States Military. Thank you for your sacrifice, your courage, and your commitment to our country.

And to the families and loved ones who keep the home fires burning. You are the heart and soul of the military.

Acknowledgements

I can finish no book without the help of the wonderful support system I have.

Brandy Walker, woman, you know that I would never be able to keep up with everything without. And yes, dammit, I LOVE those lists.

Thanks to Kris Cook, Ali Flores and Joy Harris for the wonderful Harmless in Savannah that gave me the break I needed.

Les, who still hasn't learned how to waltz, but I still love you anyway.

And to the people behind the scenes:

Kendra Egert for her wonderful cover art.

Chloe Vale who worked overtime to get the book edited and helped me with the formatting.

I could not have done this without your help. Thank you.

Infatuation

A Little Harmless Military Romance

Melissa Schroeder

Infatuation: A Little Harmless Military Romance

Edited by Chloe Vale

Cover by Kendra Egert

Formatting by Chloe Vale

First print publication: May 2012

Chapter One

The sound of Hawaiian music drifted lightly through the air as Kade took a small sip of his beer. He stood on the side of the dance floor watching the wedding guests. It was one of those days Hawaiians took for granted he was sure, but Kade didn't. The sweet scent of plumeria tickled his nose, and the sound of the ocean just a few hundred yards away combined with the music to ensure that the entire day seemed magical. The groom, Chris Dupree, smiled like a man who had just finished Hell Week with honors, while his new bride, Cynthia, glowed with more than that "happily just married" glow. Her gently rounded tummy was barely visible, but everyone knew she was pregnant.

"Never thought he would settle down," Malachi, Chris' brother, said from beside him. One of Kade's best friends, Mal had dragged him across the Pacific Ocean to make the wedding.

"Really? He's been with her for years. It only took him this long to convince her to marry, right?"

Mal laughed and took a long drink out of his bottle.

"Ain't that the truth," Mal said, New Orleans threading his voice. Their friendship was an odd one, that was for sure. Mal had grown up as part of a huge family in New Orleans, and was half creole. The name Dupree meant something in circles down there, especially in hospitality. Francis McKade grew up the child of Australian immigrants, both scientists recruited to work for the US

1

Military.

"At least there are lots of lovely ladies here for the picking," Mal said, his gaze roaming over the crowd. "There's something about Hawaiian women, you know?"

Kade said nothing but nodded. He wasn't particularly interested in most of the women today. The woman he wanted set off signs of being interested in him, but she had never acted on it.

"Are you two flipping a coin to see who gets what woman?"

The amused female voice slipped down his spine and into his blood. Before turning around, he knew who she was. Shannon Dupree, youngest sister of his best friend, and the woman who had starred in most of his most vivid sex dreams. He turned to face her, thinking he was ready for the impact, but of course he wasn't. As usual, she stole his breath away.

She was dressed in red, the main color of the wedding. The soft material draped over her generous curves. Shannon was built like Kade loved his women. Full hips, abundant breasts, and so many curves his fingers itched to explore. Every time he was near her, he had to count backwards from ten and imagine that he was taking a shower in freezing water. Sometimes that worked.

"What makes you think we're doing that?" Mal asked.

One eyebrow rose as she studied her brother. "I've known you for twenty-eight years, that's how I know."

Shannon turned to Kade expectantly, and he couldn't think. Every damned thought vaporized. It was those eyes. Green with a hint of brown, they were so unusual, and they stood out against her light brown skin. He could just imagine how they would look filled with heat and lust.

He finally cleared his throat and mentally gave himself a shake. Staring at her like a fifteen-year-old with a crush wasn't really cool. "Don't lump me in with your brother, here. He doesn't have any standards."

2

"Except for that stripper last time you visited?"

There was a beat of silence. "Stripper?"

"Mal ratted you out."

He gave his friend a nasty look. His last visit to New Orleans hadn't gone that well. Shannon had gotten very serious about her current boyfriend, and there had been talk of them moving in together. Kade had done the one thing he could to ignore the pain. He got drunk and went out to strip clubs. And Mal had been the one with the stripper, not him.

"I think your brother had that wrong."

She glanced back and forth between them. "Whatever. Just make sure you stick around for some of the reception before you go sniffing any women."

"Don't worry about me. Your brother has the impulse control problem."

Shannon laughed.

Mal grunted. "Both of you suck."

"They're going to be cutting the cake soon, so at least hold off until then, could you?"

With that she brushed past them, and he could smell her. God, she was exotic. Even with all the scents of Hawaii surrounding him, hers stood out. Spicy, sweet...

He took another pull from his longneck bottle, trying to cool his libido.

"So, who do you have in mind?" Mal asked, pulling him from his thoughts.

"What?"

"Man, it's a wedding. Women are always ripe for seduction at these things. You have to have someone in mind."

His gaze traveled back to Shannon. She walked through the crowd, her hips swaying sensually as she moved from person to person. Her smile enticed everyone she spoke to. As the owner of a bar and grill in New Orleans, she knew how to work a room. And dammit, she

had that perfect smile that drew every man to her. His hand
started to hurt, and he looked down to find his fist
clenched so tight around his bottle his knuckles were
white. It took a couple of seconds to calm himself down.
He didn't have a right to be jealous. She wasn't his to love,
to protect. He'd learned a long time ago that being a Seal
and being married just didn't work out.

He noticed Mal looking at him, expecting an answer.

"Not sure, mate, but I have a feeling I'll find someone
to occupy my time."

· · · · ·

Shannon shivered as she took a sip of champagne. She
tried not to wince at the taste. What the holy hell was she
doing drinking it? She hated the drink. What she needed
was two fingers of whiskey. It would clear her head of the
sexy Seal that had her pulse skipping.

"What are you doing drinking that?" her sister,
Jocelyn, asked.

When Shannon turned, she couldn't fight the smile.
Seeing the transformation of her sister in the last year was
amazing. Seeing her happily married with Kai added to the
joy she felt for Jocelyn. Even if there was a little jolt of
envy, Shannon couldn't begrudge her the happiness. After
the things she had overcome, Jocelyn deserved it more
than anyone she knew.

"I thought it best. You know with the jet lag and all
that, I need to keep my wits about me. Champagne should
help, right?"

Her sister's eyes danced with barely suppressed
amusement. "It couldn't be because of one hot Seal with a
hint of an Aussie accent, could it?

Shannon closed her eyes and sighed. "That man gets
my temperature up. All he has to do is smile, and I'm

ready to strip naked and jump his bones." She opened her eyes. "Is it that obvious?"

Jocelyn shook her head. "Just to someone who knows you like I do."

And no two people knew each other better. As the two girls in a huge family of men, they had depended on each other. Only fifteen months apart in age, they were more like twins than just sisters.

"Are you talking about that hot Seal your brother brought with him?" May Aiona Chambers asked as she stepped up to the two women. After meeting her just months earlier at Jocelyn's wedding, Shannon had instantly liked the sassy Hawaiian. Petite with the most amazing long hair and blue green eyes, she never seemed to have a problem voicing her opinion.

"Oh, May, please, could you join us in the conversation," Jocelyn said with a laugh.

"As my sister-in-law, you should be used to it by now." She dismissed Jocelyn and honed in on Shannon. "He's been watching you."

"What?" she asked, her voice squeaking. "No he hasn't."

"That Seal, he's been watching you all day."

Shannon snorted, trying to hide the way her heart rate jumped. "You're insane. Does this run in the family? You might want to adopt children, Jocelyn."

"No, really, he has. He does it when he thinks you aren't looking."

She turned around and found him easily on the other side of the dance floor. That erect posture made it easy. He always looked like he was standing at attention. Even in civvies, he looked like a Seal. The Hawaiian print polo shirt hugged his shoulders and was tucked neatly into his khaki dress slacks. He wasn't the tallest man in the room, but he stood out. All that hard muscle, not to mention the blond hair and the to-die-for blue eyes, made him a gorgeous package. Everything in her yearned, wanted. Of course, he wasn't looking at them. His attention was on the other side of the room. Probably on some damned stripper. Shannon turned back to her sister and May.

"Are you drunk?" Shannon asked.

May rolled her eyes. "No, really he has. You know what those Seals are like. He can do surveillance without you knowing. It's his job. But you should see the way he looks at you."

She couldn't help herself. "Like how?"

May hummed. "Like he wants to take a big, long bite out of you."

She couldn't stop the shiver that slinked down her spine or the way her body heated at the thought. Since she had met him five years earlier, she had been interested in him. He was quiet, unlike her brothers, and the way he moved…God, she knew for sure he was good in bed. But it was more than that. Kade was sexy, that was for sure, but there was something more to him than just a good-looking man. There was an innate goodness in him, one that made a woman know he would take care of her no matter what.

"If I were you, I would make use of the event to get him in bed."

Shannon snorted again, trying to keep herself from imagining it—and failing. "Please, May, tell me what you really think."

"Believe me, I know about waiting, and it isn't worth it. I waited years for some idiot to notice me. I think of all the time we wasted dancing around like that."

"Did you just call your husband an idiot?" Jocelyn asked.

May rolled her eyes. "He overlooked me for years, then waited forever once he did notice me. Of course he's an idiot. But in this situation, you have to be strategic. I saw Evan almost every day. This guy, he's going to be gone again with that job of his. You have got to take advantage of the wedding and get him into bed. Get a little wedding booty."

She should be mad, but it was hard to be. May looked so innocent with her sweet smile, and her voice sounded like something out of a movie. Shannon just couldn't get irritated with her. Before May could say anything else, they announced the cutting of the cake. She turned to face the banquet table, and as she did, she caught Kade looking at her. It was the briefest moment, just a second, but even across all that space, she saw the heat, the longing, and felt it build inside of her. Her breath backed up in her lungs. In that next instant, he looked away.

It took all her power to turn her attention back to the event at hand, seeing her brother and her sister-in-law beaming at each other, she took another sip of champagne. May was right. She had to take a chance. If he said no, if he ignored her, then she could drink herself in a stupor and have months before she had to face him again.

But there was one thing Shannon Michele Dupree did right, and that was being bold. She chugged the rest of her champagne, set it on the table next to her, and headed off in Kade's direction.

That man wouldn't know what hit him.

Chapter Two

Kade's heart jumped into his throat when he saw Shannon walking determinedly in his direction. She wore her hair up to show off her slender neck and the diamond earrings he knew Mal had bought her. God, she was gorgeous. He liked strong women, and that was definitely Shannon. All the feminine strength in that sexy package, he was having a hard time resisting her. Everything in his body, especially one particular body part, told him to go after her. But his brain wouldn't let him. He couldn't act on his attraction. Mal was his best friend, and one of the things he'd always believed in was you didn't fuck around with your buddy's sister. Since Kade knew he wasn't cut out to be involved for the long haul, he had to ignore the lust that was circling his gut right now.

Damn, as she neared, he saw she was coming after him for something. What had he done? With Shannon, you never knew what would happen. The woman ran a tight ship at work, and no one, not even her trained-to-kill Navy Seal brother, got away with jack shit with her.

"Hey, Kade," she said just as the band started up with a slow country song. Even with the music playing, he could hear her accent. "Do you think you could dance a little two-step with me? I know you have to be one of the only guys here who knows how to do it right."

The way she said it made him think of sex. Who was he fooling? Everything she said made him think of sex. But now, she was smiling, those green eyes sparkling up at him, and he couldn't think again.

"What?"

She laughed. The sound of it sunk into his blood and made his pulse do its own two-step. "Dance. You, me. Two-step. You haven't forgotten how to do it, have you?"

The memory of her teaching him to two-step filtered through his mind. It had felt like purgatory, stuck between heaven and hell. Her body had moved against his, her soft breasts pressed against his chest...he'd almost lost it. The only thing that had saved him was that Mal was on that very same dance floor and probably would have beaten the hell out of him if he had known what Kade was thinking.

"Uh...yeah, I remember."

She didn't wait for a yes or no. She just grabbed his hand and dragged him behind her to the dance floor. She stopped then waited for him to step closer. Kade hesitated, trying to get his brain back into the game. Of course, his little brain wanted to do most of the thinking. His cock twitched as he drew her into his arms. They started to dance, and he tried to keep her further away. She slipped closer.

Oh, shit. Just the little brush of her body against his had his cock hardening. He just hoped she didn't notice.

"I thought you and Mal would be off having a good old time."

He glanced down at her, wondering about the tone. There was a thread of irritation in it. She was smiling up at him as if there was nothing wrong, but he knew there was something she wasn't telling him.

"Apparently your brother had a woman picked out already."

She nodded. "He's a slut."

Kade couldn't help it. He threw back his head and laughed. Shannon had a way of talking about her brothers, especially Mal, that Kade knew was to remind them they were still just her brothers.

9

"What about you?" she asked.

"I'm not a slut."

She chuckled. "The jury's still out on that one."

"Your brother needs to learn how to be a little more picky."

Her lips curved up at that comment, and he felt the moisture dry up in his mouth. God, he wanted to kiss that smile off her face—then move down her body, exploring every delicious inch of her. He knew her flesh would be sweet.

"I noticed you're pretty picky."

He nodded as he worked her around the dance floor. "I don't fall for every pretty face that comes along."

She said nothing. Instead she laid her head on his shoulder. The gesture was so natural it was as if she did it every day. He knew he should tell her not to. His brain said he should do it. But he couldn't. It was too close to what he wanted, what he yearned for. For five long years he had wanted her, wanted to feel this way with her, her head on his shoulder, her soft, warm body in his arms. He had wanted that for so long, he just couldn't bring himself to stop her.

It was bad enough he would probably have to take a five-hour cold shower when he got back to the room. Sweat slid down his back, and he had to fight the urge to lean down and brush his lips over her forehead.

He had talked himself into not doing more when she sighed and relaxed even more against him. Her breasts were pressed against his chest, and with every breath he drew in that sultry scent that was so unique to her. His head started to spin. His body started to duel with his mind. His brain was starting to lose when the music ended. The band swung into a fast-paced Hawaiian tune. His body protested when he had to pull back.

"Shannon?"

Even to his own ears, his voice sounded gruff. She

raised her head and blinked as if coming out of some kind of daze. Her breathing hitched, and her breasts rose above the neckline of her dress. His gaze slipped down, he could see her hardened nipples through the delicate red fabric. He curled his fingers into his palms and counted backwards from ten. If he didn't get away from her soon, he would definitely lose control. There would be nothing to stop him from tearing off her clothes and bending her over a banquet table.

The wind shifted, pulling a few strands of her hair loose from the complicated style.

He cleared his throat. "Well, that was...nice."

Fuck. How lame could he get? She studied him for a second, her expression serious, thoughtful. Then in the next moment, her lips curved.

"You know where my room is, doncha?"

Lust soared. His body reacted at the direct question. Any doubts he had about her interest in him vaporized. She apparently thought there was no reason to hide her attraction to him anymore.

He nodded, unable to form a word.

"Well, then you know where to find me later."

With that, she walked away, and he couldn't help watching her hips and that magnificent ass of hers. He could just imagine having her on all fours in front of him as he took her from behind.

Kade drew in a deep breath. He needed to get a drink. He needed to go away, far away. He could not breach the trust his friend put in him. If another man had thoughts about his sister like he had about Shannon, well, he would kill him. Of course, his sister was married with five kids, so there was a really good chance his brother-in-law had those thoughts.

He headed over to the bar. After ordering another beer, he turned and found himself face to face with Kai Aiona, Shannon's brother-in-law.

"Hey, man. I saw you out there with Shannon."

"Yeah. I've known all the Duprees for a long time."

He nodded. "Those two women, though, they melt a man's brain."

He didn't know what else to say, so he just nodded and took a shallow sip off his bottle.

Kai laughed. "Don't worry, bra. I won't be bugging you about your intentions. The one thing I understand about the Dupree women is that they have their own minds. Just make sure you know what you're about. I'd hate to have to beat the crap out of you to make Jocelyn happy."

"I'm a Seal."

Kai laughed in his face again. "And I've been working on the docks since I was a teen."

They eyed each other, and Kade realized he'd come up against an adversary he might not be able to beat. He wasn't as muscular as Kade, but there was something to be said about a man who knew how to fight dirty.

"Now, speaking of my bride, I need to hunt her up. We have a big suite to use for the night."

He left Kade alone to his thoughts. He didn't have to look for Shannon, he knew where she was. It didn't matter if he tried to ignore her, he could always sense where she was if she was nearby. He could find her in a crowd of a thousand. He watched as she pulled May and Kai's father out onto the dance floor and tried to teach him to two-step. It was silly that his heart turned over just at the sight of her. She was smiling as usual, her joy easy to see. Shannon enjoyed life, every little bit of it, to the fullest extent. Out of all of the Duprees, she was the one who could always find a silver lining in any cloud. And now she had pulled away the barriers he'd thought were there. She had made her interest clear.

As he watched her dance, he felt his resistance melt. He might not have the right, but the lady had given him an invitation, and even if it was for just this one night, he would taste a little bit of paradise.

With his job, there were few opportunities for it. Once—just this once—he would take the chance.

. . . . .

Shannon looked at herself in the mirror and drew in a deep breath. She looked good. No, correct that. She looked damned hot. The dress Cynthia had picked out for her had been fantastic. Red was definitely her color, and the design suited her fuller figure. Best of all, it was a dress she could wear again. And she would. Either to remind her of a great night, or remind her not to have stupid yearnings that would never come true.

She groaned and grabbed a bottle of water. After taking a swig, she hoped that it helped cool off her raging libido. If history served, nothing would help. Not even her battery-operated boyfriend could relieve the fire that man started in her. She closed her eyes and tried to calm her heart. Just thinking about Kade had her body humming with anticipation. She was already driving herself crazy, and she had only been in her room twenty minutes. It took all of her control not to pace the room. It would be stupid to worry herself over the invitation she'd given Kade. Seriously, she didn't expect him to show. Hoped, but didn't really think it would happen.

Oh, there was no doubt he wanted her. A man didn't get that hard by just dancing unless he wanted a woman or had just had a handful of the blue pills. Shannon was pretty damned sure that Francis McKade didn't need them.

She stepped out onto her balcony and looked out over the water. The scent of salt filled her senses. She loved it in Hawaii. She would never be able to leave New Orleans, but she definitely liked it in Chris's adopted home. While her hometown was always abuzz with activity, something she loved, she did like the slower pace of the islands. She liked to come here and gaze out over the water and just...breathe.

But even that didn't work. Being in the same hotel as Kade, she couldn't think of anything else other than seeing him in her room, preferably naked. She needed something to occupy her time. If she didn't, she would definitely tear into the bag of chocolate macadamia nuts. Her ass didn't need that.

She watched the surf as it rolled in, and she could see why her brother and sister had been drawn to Hawaii. This was a soothing place. Oahu could be a jungle, that was for sure, but there was something so...relaxed. She could never live here. It would take an act of war to get her out of New Orleans. She had rebuilt her bar after Katrina, and she wasn't leaving any time soon. But she needed to find time to return to Hawaii. She had a niece or nephew about to make an appearance, and she was sure Jocelyn and Kai would have children soon.

A little ping hit her heart harder than it ever had before. Thinking of her sister, her confidant, having a baby brought about yearnings she never thought she would have, not now. She thought they would come after marriage, but it was probably because the first Dupree grandchild would be arriving in five months.

Shannon shook herself free of her funk. This wasn't like her. She had men. Not a constant stream of them, and she did have the problem of her career. Her business took up a fair amount of her time, so it had been a long dry spell between men. But for some reason, she hadn't felt the need to scratch the itch. Not until she saw her brother coming down the escalator at the airport with Kade.

She closed her eyes and shivered. Damn, the man got to her. And if he didn't take her up on her offer, she would write him off. His loss. She opened her eyes and glanced at the ABC Drugstore bag. She would throw away the condoms she bought and drink whiskey and eat the chocolate.

There was a knock at the door, pulling her out of thoughts of rebellion by gorging herself. She drew in a deep breath and approached the door. When she looked through the peephole, she sighed. It was an older Asian man. She opened it, and he looked confused.

The door across the hall opened, and a woman who was apparently his wife frowned at him.

"Sorry," he said with a smile.

"No problem," Shannon said, trying to fight the disappointment that now swamped her as she watched his wife usher him into their room. She was closing the door when a hand braced against it and stopped her. She looked up and found Kade staring at her.

"I told you I knew where your room was."

His voice flowed over the words. He had been born in Australia, but his parents had moved to the US when he was younger. That accent still tinged his voice. It sent little tingles of heat racing through her blood.

"You didn't change your mind, did you?"

He actually looked worried. The fact that he would think any woman in her right mind wouldn't beg him to come to her room made him even more attractive.

She smiled and stepped back. "Come on in, Kade."

Chapter Three

As Kade watched Shannon step back, he tried to calm his heart. It was smacking against his chest so hard he was sure she heard it. Lust hummed through his body. He was afraid if he didn't control himself, he would completely lose it, strip her naked, and ride her like she was a mare in heat.

"Kade?" she asked.

He shook himself out of the stupor as he stepped over the threshold and shut the door behind himself. He flipped the deadbolt and took her in his arms. Somewhere in the back of his mind, he realized he was rushing, but he couldn't help it. He couldn't be that controlled when he kissed her. He had waited too long to touch, to taste. She didn't hesitate, but came willingly into his arms and pressed herself against him. *Lord*. His eyes almost crossed at the feel of all that softness against him. Her nipples were hard.

He kissed her then, taking her lips in a hot, open-mouthed kiss. She was better than he dreamed. As he dove into her mouth, she hummed against his tongue. Every hormone in his body screamed, begging for relief, but there was one thing he knew. He might never get to do this again, and if so, he would make sure this would last him a lifetime.

He kissed a path down her neck, enjoying the taste of her flesh. God, she was so sweet. She arched into him, and he swore. He almost came then and there. No woman had ever gotten to him like this. He pulled away.

"Turn around."

His voice was rough, and he saw that her eyes widened slightly. When she did as he ordered, she did it slowly, her hips swaying as she turned. The woman was going to drive him insane. There was no doubt about it. His hands were shaking when he lifted them to unzip the dress. He was careful not to jerk the delicate fabric, but it was hard. As the fabric spilt, it revealed a black lace corset, stockings, and mother help him, a thong.

She was definitely going to kill him. Blood rushed to his groin, and his head started to spin again. The dress fell away and pooled on the floor at her feet. When she turned around, his eyes almost crossed.

The corset was tight, pushing her generous breasts up to the edge and almost over the top. The stockings were attached by garters. As he allowed his gaze to drift down, he had to sigh. She was made for him. There was no doubt in his mind. He didn't like thin women, disdained them. He liked a handful of a woman. One who knew her worth and who had more curves than he could explore in a lifetime.

"Kade?"

He could barely hear her voice. He lifted his hand and skimmed the tips of his fingers over the delicate flesh above the lace. She shivered then moaned as he slipped his digit between her breasts.

"Kade?"

He looked up at her and the frown she was giving him. "Don't say no now."

She smiled at that. "Not on your life, it's just that…you have a lot of clothes on. I'm almost naked."

He didn't do anything. He couldn't. He was still trying to come to terms with the fact that the woman he had lusted after for so long was standing in front of him in a corset.

He swore then that he was positive there was a God.

Apparently, she got sick of waiting. Shannon stepped forward and took hold of his shirt.

"Arms up, Seal."

He did as ordered, unable to fight the smile curving his lips. He knew it would be like this. Softness, tenderness, fun, and love. She tossed the shirt behind her and immediately had her hands on his chest.

"Lord, you Seals know how to build some muscles."

The wonder in her voice shot straight to his dick. She splayed her hands over his pecs and smoothed them over his flesh. He was sure she could feel the way his heart pounded against his chest.

"I like that you aren't all waxed."

He snorted. "No military man would do so, babe."

Her gaze flashed up to his. "Yeah? I bet there are a few."

"Let me rephrase that. No self-respecting Seal would wax."

"Ah," she said and nodded as she slipped her hands up over his shoulders. The lace of her corset scratched against his skin, and he was amazed he didn't lose consciousness. There was so much he wanted to do to her, with her. But he couldn't go into full Dom mode, not with Shannon. Tonight was more about sharing, caring, and living in the moment.

He bent his head and kissed her. This time he wasn't so out of control. Slowly he tasted her, nipping at her lips, then finally he delved into her mouth. He walked her back to the bed until her legs hit it. He pulled back and pushed her a little. She took the hint and fell on the bed, a laugh bubbling up from within her. That joy was something he would remember for the rest of his life. He didn't doubt it.

She was laying on the bed, her hair tousled around her head now, and that sexy smile inviting him to join her. He did then, undoing her corset and garters. He slipped the

lace from her body, but he didn't remove the stockings.
Next he worked the tiny thong down her legs. It was wet
with her arousal, the musky scent of it sending his libido to
new heights. He kissed the flesh just above the band of the
stocking, then the other leg. He worked his way up to her
sex. She was hot, and damn, so wet.

Need crawled through him, urging him to take, to
plunder. He couldn't control himself, couldn't wait. He
had to have a taste of her. He set his mouth against her
pussy and leisurely licked her. She shivered and moaned
against him.

He savored her, slipping his tongue inside of her and
allowing the flavor of her to dance over his taste buds.
God, every little bit of her was exquisite, inside and out.
Adding a finger, he enjoyed the way her muscles clamped
down on it as he worked in and out of her. He could just
imagine sliding inside, having those inner pussy walls
tugging on his cock. He sighed against her as he slipped
his tongue up and over her clit.

She shivered, moving against him. He sensed her
approaching orgasm and pulled away.

She moaned in irritation and gave him a dirty look. He
laughed and worked his way up her torso, kissing and
licking her sweet skin. When he reached her breasts, he
took one hardened nipple into his mouth and
sucked—hard. She moaned again, slipping her hands into
his hair as he slid his other hand to her breast and teased
the nipple.

Little by little, she was killing him. Pleasure took hold
of his body, of his mind. At this point, he wasn't sure how
much longer he would last. He was a man who loved
foreplay. He thought with Shannon he would take hours.
He had dreamed of it for years, planned it. Then when she
was so out of her mind she was begging for relief, he
would take her.

There was no way he would make it. He didn't have

the ability to take it slow. If he tried, there was a good chance he would embarrass himself.

She arched up against him, pressing her crotch against his pants. Even through the cotton fabric, he felt her heat. He knew then it was imperative that he got naked ASAP.

He gave her breast one last lick, then he rose to his knees. He was ready to undress, but apparently she was sick of waiting. She sat up and took over the job herself. He didn't wear underwear, so when she unzipped him, his straining cock sprung free. Her eyes widened, and she wrapped her hand around it.

"Oh, Shannon, yeah..."

His words trailed off as he lost the ability to speak. He watched her dip her head and take the tip of his penis into her mouth. The first flick of her tongue pulled a drop of pre-come from him. He shuddered, and he knew he should tell her to stop. There was every chance that he would lose it, lose complete control and come right then in there. But instead, he watched as his cock disappeared between her lips and into the deep recesses of her mouth. It was possibly one of the most erotic things he had ever seen.

She took it slowly at first, just pulling in about half of his cock. But soon he was thrusting in and out of her mouth, and she was humming against his sensitive flesh.

He pulled away right about the time he lost it. It was when he looked down at her that he realized he hadn't brought protection.

Shit.

Before he could say anything, Shannon solved the problem. "In the bag on the table."

He noticed the plastic bag then. He jumped off the bed, got rid of his pants, and pulled out the box of condoms. His hands were shaking with desire, and he could barely get the box open as he crawled back up on the bed. When he did, the condoms went flying all over the bed beside her. She laughed, the joy of it loosening something in his heart. As he looked down at her, he couldn't believe that this woman, with her loving nature and her beauty, wanted him.

"I don't know about you, but that seems pretty ambitious. But you *are* the first Seal I've gone to bed with."

He looked at the condoms and couldn't fight the gurgle of laughter. He grabbed one. "I don't like to waste anything, so we better get started, babe."

He ripped open the condom and had it on in record time. He wanted it fast and hard, but he knew he couldn't push her. He would probably have to leave in the next few hours, knowing his luck. So he decided he would at least try and take it slow.

He slipped his hands over her belly, enjoying the way her muscles quivered beneath his palm. So soft, so silky, her skin amazed him. He would never get enough of her, he knew that much. He slid his hands to her hips and pulled her up. With one hard thrust, he entered her. At first he worried he had been too hard, but the next moment she moaned. The sound of it filled the quiet room and filtered into his soul. He started to move, tried to keep himself in check. He was a man who was known for his control, but where Shannon was concerned, he barely had any.

It didn't take her long. She was coming apart beneath him, and he couldn't stop his own orgasm. Her muscles clamped down hard on his cock, pulling him deeper into her warmth, and he lost himself. With one long, hard thrust, he came, shuddering as he moaned her name.

He collapsed on top of her. She grunted then laughed and wrapped her arms around him. He leaned up and looked down at her. Fuck, there wasn't a more beautiful woman. Oh, physically, plastic surgeons had perfected the female face. But never once had he seen a woman who produced such joy. He had seen some horrible things in his life, and being with her lightened his load.

21

"You really are too beautiful for me," he said, embarrassed by the way his voice had roughened.

"Oh, really? I will have you know that you and Mal were the topic of discussion among many of the women. Two hot—not my description of Mal, but theirs—Seals... I am the lucky one here."

He couldn't tell her how he felt. There were thoughts in his mind, things that he should say, but he didn't know how to put it into words. Hell, Kade wasn't really sure what he felt. All he knew was that his heart was in his throat and that the man he was an hour ago no longer existed. Not after this. He had known it would be good, but Kade hadn't known exactly how much this would mean to him. He'd had great sex before, but this was something else.

"Kade?"

He heard the worry in her voice and could say nothing to ease them. He knew he had to look too serious for the situation. Instead, he kissed her, pulling her bottom lip between his teeth. She closed her eyes and hummed. After a few minutes of teasing, he rolled off her and went to the bathroom to discard his condom. When he stepped out of the bathroom, he smiled. Shannon was already snuggled under the covers, half asleep. She was notorious for being a heavy sleeper, and someone who could fall asleep at the drop of a hat.

He walked as quietly as possible and slipped into bed. His heart turned over when she shifted closer and snuggled against him. Damn, this was more than he expected, more than he was able to give. But for this night, before the reality of the world returned, he would pretend she was his to keep forever.

Tomorrow would come soon enough.

Chapter Four

Shannon awoke slowly, blinking in the darkness. As usual, the first sense that really took hold was her sense of smell. There was a strange combination of plumeria and musky male that had her confused. It took her a second to remember just where she was.

Hawaii. Chris and Cynthia's wedding. She shifted her weight and came up against a hard wall of muscle.

Kade.

No wonder the bed felt like a heater. The man gave off heat like a steam engine. But she didn't care. She had Francis McKade in her bed.

She smiled. She knew she looked smug, but who wouldn't? The man she had in bed had to be every heterosexual woman's dream come true. As her eyes adjusted to the darkness, she pulled herself up and rested her weight on her elbow. The man was amazing. Never in her life had she had a man that looked like this in her bed. Hard muscles, tattoos on his back, and damn, but he was like a wonderland made just for her. He was as gorgeous on the inside as on the outside.

Her fingers itched to touch, to explore. They were both tired from their trips over the Pacific, but she couldn't stop herself. Without hesitation, she gave into her compulsion to touch him.

The moment she touched him, she felt that connection. It had been there from the first and had grown each time she saw him. Now there was something telling her that this was the man for her, the one that could be forever. But sadly, she didn't think it would happen. His work, her life, it wouldn't work out between the two of them.

She brushed those unhappy thoughts away and slipped her hand down his torso. She shivered at the feel of his warm flesh beneath her fingertips. Could a man be in better shape? She didn't think so. His abs were sculpted, and even without trying, she was pretty sure she could bounce a quarter off his ass.

To get a better look at him, she slipped the sheet away from his body. The moonlight was weak, but she could see him. He was tan everywhere. How did he do that? She knew without a doubt he didn't go to a tanning salon. She looked at the scar on his hip. It was a puckered wound, not very big. She knew a year or so ago, he'd been shot. Mal had told her just that and nothing else.

She grazed her finger over it and then continued down. He had a thin line of hair all the way down to his cock. As she neared it with her hands, it twitched. She glanced up at him and realized she had awakened him. His eyes were barely opened, but he was watching her. The intensity in them was a little scary and very arousing.

"Sorry," she whispered.

His lips curled up on one side. "No problem. Use and abuse me any way you want to."

"Yeah?"

He nodded.

She didn't break eye contact with him as she wrapped her hand around his cock. His eyes closed, and he groaned as she gave it one long stroke. He shifted against the bed as she continued to tease him. Soon, though, that wasn't enough. She wanted a taste. Slipping down the bed, she settled between his legs and took him in her mouth. The first taste of him spurred her arousal. Sweet and salty, with a touch of Kade, so unique, like the man. At first she couldn't fit him in her mouth completely, but soon she

24

didn't care that she gagged once or twice. It didn't seem to bother him. His groans were growing in volume, and he was shifting against her, thrusting into her mouth. She slipped her fingers down to his sac and began to stroke him. Power coursed through her veins as she continued to tease him. She knew he was close. To make him lose control would be the ultimate conquest, but apparently Kade wasn't going to allow it. He pulled her up and switched their positions. She found herself on her back, pinned to the mattress.

"You trying to be naughty, Shannon?" His voice was a guttural whisper, filled with so much arousal she could barely control the lust pouring into her veins. He loomed over her as if he was in charge, and well, it was the truth.

"I thought I was being pretty obvious." Her voice sounded breathless, but it was nothing new. He always did that to her.

His eyes sparkled with a bit of devilment, and she felt her heart skip a beat. "Yeah? Well, I think you deserve some punishment for that."

He rose to his knees, straddling her hips, his cock lying against her sex. Already she was hot, needy, and from the look in his eyes, he was going to make sure she was out of her mind. For a second he looked at her, then shook his head. He reached over to turn on the light.

"No—"

He ignored her. When he had the light on, he returned to his position. "Got a problem with light, babe? You shouldn't, not with a body like this."

He brushed his hands up her stomach, grazing the sides of her breasts, then teasing her nipples with his thumbs. She sucked in a deep breath and moaned as she closed her eyes. She had very sensitive breasts, and just the simple teasing had her pussy dampening.

"Like that, do you?"

He didn't wait for an answer. Instead, he placed a hand

on the bed beside her and leaned down to take a nipple in
his mouth. The graze of his teeth against the tip sent heat
straight to her pussy. Damn, the man was going to kill her.
The way he was straddling her, she couldn't move her
legs. The pressure built as he continued to suck one, then
both nipples. Her body was hot, her heart beating so hard
that she wasn't too sure she would survive. When he was
done there, he started to move down her body, licking and
nipping at her skin. She moved against him, and he
stopped.

"Now, naughty girl, you can't move."

She opened her eyes and frowned at him. When she
opened her mouth to respond, he placed one finger against
her mouth.

"You're the one who awoke the beast, so you get to
live with the consequences."

She wanted to tell him to go to hell, but there was
something so...sexy about him commanding her, telling
her what she could and could not do. Unlike her brother,
Chris, she had never been into BDSM, but with Kade, the
possibility was titillating. And dammit, arousal deepened
his accent. That alone made her toes curl.

He apparently took her silence as agreement. "If you
agree, I'll reward you. If not, I'll stop. And you will regret
it."

She nodded, not knowing which would be better—the
reward or the punishment? Which would be worse?

He traced her lips with his finger. The callus felt odd
against her mouth. "No coming unless I say so."

She agreed with another nod. Then he tortured her.
Slowly, he worked his way down her body. She had never
known a man so skilled with his tongue. Who would have
thought that a tongue could arouse her by just flicking over
her flesh, dipping into her belly button? By the time he
settled between her legs, she was pretty sure he'd touched
every inch of her stomach.

He drew in a deep breath, closing his eyes. Then he sighed. When he looked up at her, the need in his gaze had her breath tangling in her chest. In all her encounters, she had never had a man stare at her with such yearning. Tears burned the backs of her eyes as she tried to control her emotions. To know she was that special to him, that this was that special to him, made her want to cry happy tears.

"I'll never get over how you smell. Every bit of you is delicious," he said.

He lowered his head, and without taking his gaze from hers, he set his mouth on her sex. He used his fingers to part her labia and slid his tongue into her. At that moment, she gave into the man, allowing him complete control. She was already halfway there to begin with, but now, he had her body doing whatever he wanted. She would give anything to come, to be allowed to have her release. In and out he worked his tongue, lapping at her as if she were a delicious treat he adored. He slipped two fingers into her as he began to tease her clit. He rolled his tongue over the tiny bundle of nerves, then between his teeth, gently pressing down. Pressure soared, her body shivered with her impending orgasm. She felt the rush of heat flood her sex, but he pulled back. She made a noise that was halfway between a growl and a moan.

"I didn't say you could come."

She wanted to yell at him, but he gently slapped her pussy. The act would get a normal man yelled at, but he had her so aroused, ribbons of lust slipped over her flesh and down into her bones at the action. He did it again, and her body responded even more willingly.

"Damn," he said. Without explanation, he set his mouth against her, slipping his hands beneath her rear end and pulling her up. Relentlessly, he assaulted her senses, pushing her almost to the pinnacle but pulling back just in time to keep her from reaching it. Over and over he teased, pushing her right up to the edge, but not allowing her relief. She moved against him, pressing her cunt as hard as she could against his mouth. The way he was holding her, she really couldn't get leverage.

By the time he lifted his head and set her down on the mattress, she was out of her mind. The only thing she could think of was release. She would do anything to feel the rush of her orgasm.

He slipped his fingers into her sex. "Come for me, baby. Do it."

The order sent her spiraling into her orgasm. Her body convulsed as she screamed as ripples of euphoria washed over her. She could do nothing else. She arched off the bed and allowed the orgasm to take over. Just as she was coming down, he sent her over again as she writhed against his hand.

She was still shivering moments later when he grabbed a condom and donned it. Without any words, he flipped her over onto her stomach, pulled her up to her knees, and entered her from behind. His hands gripped her hips as he thrust in and out of her with such force that the headboard banged against the wall. After her two intense orgasms, she thought another would be impossible, but he smacked her ass. The action sent a mixture of pleasure and pain. He did it again, thrusting even harder into her, and she screamed as another release slammed through her. After a few more thrusts, he shouted her name and followed her.

Several minutes later, he pulled out of her, got rid of the condom, then settled beside her on the bed. He pulled her into his arms, and she cuddled closer.

"Hoo-rah," he said, his voice filled with sleepy satisfaction.

"I have to say I agree, Seal."

He chuckled then kissed her forehead. It was sweet, not sexual at all, but it had a lump filling up her throat. She slipped her hand up to his chest, could feel his heart beat against it. Shannon tried to stay awake, wanting to savor

every moment they had together, but soon his even
breathing relaxed her, and she drifted into sleep.

· · · · ·

The sun was barely peeking through the curtains when
Anchors Aweigh woke Shannon from a dead sleep. She
heard Kade curse then grab the phone.

"Yes, sir, McKade here."

He was silent as he listened for a moment or two.

"Understood. Have you talked to Dupree?" He waited.
"Okay. Expect us on the next plane we can get out of
here."

He turned off the phone and glanced at her. "Gotta go."

She nodded. As the sister of a Seal, she understood.
She knew there would be no discussion about where he
was going, what he was doing. And he had no control over
what would go down and when.

She gave him a kiss. "I understand. Did he talk to
Mal?"

Kade studied her for a second. "Yes. So, more than
likely, he'll be looking for me."

Again, he was studying her, and she couldn't stand it
any longer. "What?"

"I...I thought we might have more time."

She sighed. "You might want to have more time, but
you know the military. You get what you can and be happy
for that."

She couldn't look at him, not right now. It hurt too
much to think of him going away, of being in danger.
Shannon had been through this before with both Mal and
Kade, but this time was so much different. This time she
had so much more to lose.

He slipped his finger under her chin. "Don't be mad."

She frowned. "I'm not mad. I just hate thinking of both

of you in danger."

He nodded and gave her a soft, quick kiss. It was really innocent, but she felt the heat, the need behind it. It curled her toes and had her heart turning over. Then it turned hot, his tongue slipping between her lips and stealing into her mouth. Kade started to ease her back, but she stopped him. He pulled back just far enough to talk.

"What?" he asked.

"Don't you have to find a flight?"

"It can wait." His lips curved. "I need one more taste of heaven."

The way he said it had her resistance crumbling. As she allowed him to ease her back onto the bed, she told herself to enjoy the moment. There was time enough to fall to pieces after he left.

Chapter Five

Four months later

"When did he say he was going to be here?" Verna asked as she settled against the barstool.

Shannon looked at her. She saw the expectant look on her employee's face and inwardly cringed. Damn Mal for flirting with her employees. Verna didn't hold a torch for him, but since his last visit, Shannon could tell Verna had been itching to get her hands all over him. If he chased off another employee, she was going to shave his eyebrows off.

"Not sure. He's driving in."

"Kade's not coming?" Verna asked.

Shannon couldn't help but feel the sharp slash at her heart. Verna didn't mean anything because no one, as far as Shannon knew, had guessed she'd spent Kade's last night in Hawaii with him. Almost every time Mal had come into town in the last few years, Kade had come with him.

"Not that I know of."

She finished wiping down the counter and walked back to her office, not wanting to talk anymore about Mal's visit. It was a slow night. Off-season in New Orleans and the weather sucked. A bad storm had hit just thirty minutes earlier, which meant they would probably be left with no customers. Seemed like everyone was staying in. She shut the office door and then collapsed into her desk chair. With a sigh, she indulged in a little pity.

Four months and no word from Kade.

When he had left, he had said he would get in touch. And he had. There had been a few texts, two calls, then nothing. She tried not to panic. After years of Mal in the

Seals, she knew exactly how it went. This time was different. Her worry had kept her up at night and rode on her shoulder during the day. Probably because she had no one to talk to about it. She hadn't even told her sister what had happened the night of Chris's wedding.

She had known they were back because Mal had called to tell her both of them had been injured. Mal had played it off, as usual, but she had sensed something had gone wrong. They had lost one member of the team. It had hit them all hard, she was sure. What she didn't understand was why Kade had not called. It wasn't like him at all. Even if it had just been a one-night stand, it wasn't like them to stay away this long. She had worked through the pain and anger, and now...she just wanted an answer. But she apparently wasn't going to get it. Her texts and calls were still being ignored. Whatever she thought they had shared had been an illusion, or possibly just one-sided.

Before she could get too depressed, she heard her brother's voice booming out from the bar area.

"Where is my gorgeous sister?"

Excitement had her jumping up from the chair and running out to see him. He was drenched, but he had a big smile on his face and his arms open wide. She didn't hesitate, didn't think to. The entire family was close, and these last few months had been hard on all of them. She ran to him and jumped into his arms. Tears stung the back of her eyes as he hugged her tight.

"It's so good to see you," she said just loud enough for him to hear. Her voice wavered a bit, and she was afraid she just might start crying.

He gave her one last squeeze and then pulled back. Up close, she could see a new scar on his lip.

"Bad assignment?" she asked and was embarrassed that her voice caught.

He nodded. "But I came out of it with flying colors. Not like the losers I brought with me."

He motioned with his head behind him, and she followed the direction. There, on the steps leading down into her bar, stood Kade. A rush of relief came first, her heart now happier to know that he really was okay. She knew Mal wouldn't have lied about something major, but he might have hidden the injuries Kade had suffered.

In the next instant, irritation replaced it. There he stood in her bar, larger than life, if a little more ragged around the edge. Dammit, he should look apologetic. Still, she couldn't say anything. Not with an audience.

"You know Kade, of course," Mal said, his voice dipping a bit in a threatening way. She glanced at him, wondering if he had guessed what had gone on, but if he did, he hid it well. "I don't believe you've met Chief."

She realized that there was another man there beside Kade. She guessed he was older than both Mal and Kade by just a few years. Tall, blond, he was assessing the room like most of the Seals she'd met. His gaze roamed over her customers. He had his arm in a sling, telling her more than just Mal and Kade had been injured. When he focused his attention on her, she felt it to her toes. His gray eyes were as intense as the man. Damn, these men were dangerous.

"Chief," she said.

"Deke, ma'am."

She smiled. "Then you must call me Shannon."

He looked at her for a second, then a slow, sexy smile curled his lips. Dangerous was too simple of a word for the Viking god standing in front of her.

"Certainly."

Mal made a disgusted sound. "That's enough of that."

She hadn't truly looked at Kade until now. He hadn't said a word. Now, though, she turned her attention to him. If it had not been melodramatic, she would have gasped. He'd lost weight. He had a fresh scar above his right eye, and his eyes, those beautiful blue eyes, were cold. The sparkle was gone. He offered her no smile. As she allowed

33

her gaze to drop, she noticed he was favoring his right leg.

"Hey, Kade."

He hesitated. "Hey."

She could barely hear him above the noise in the bar. His voice was low and gravelly and very un-Kade-like.

"I was hoping that you had room to spare for us," Mal said.

Shannon tore her attention away from Kade and looked at her brother. He was smiling at her with the same puppy dog eyes that made most women melt. Not his sister. She was ready to say no and send them to her mother. She didn't need to deal with three injured surly men, especially one who had just about broken her heart. But there was something else in Mal's expression, something a little desperate. Their mama could fit them, and she would definitely fatten Kade up and baby the three of them. For some reason, though, Mal wanted to be with her.

She nodded. "Sure. You know my house is big enough for y'all."

Mal kissed her cheek. "Do you have to close up?"

"No, she doesn't," Simon, her bartender said. He was watching her like a hawk, and she knew that he sensed her hesitation. "Go on, boss. I can handle this."

She smiled. "Thanks. I'll just get my things."

Mal nodded.

"You know the way and you have a key. I'll catch up with you in a minute," she said.

He ushered the other two out. She felt Kade give her a look, but she couldn't return it. Her emotions were too raw, too...unbalanced. She didn't know what she would do. If she did, she would surely yell or cry. Or both.

She walked back to her office with Simon on her heels.

"So that's the guy."

She glanced back at one of her best friends and sighed. She should have known that he would figure it out.

"What are you talking about?"

34

"You've been moping around since you returned from the wedding."

"I have not," she said, lying through her teeth as she pretended to shut down the computer.

"Yeah, sure. This is Simon, child."

She sighed and looked at him. He was a year older than her and ten times prettier. Long brown hair, blue eyes, and a dimple in his chin made him irresistible to both men and women. Being the tramp that he was, Simon had no problem with either of them.

"Simon, how many times do I have to tell you that you're white? *Really* white. When you talk like that, you sound stupid."

He rolled his eyes. "And you're stalling because you don't want to answer me."

"Yes, he's the reason I have been out of sorts."

Simon snorted. "Yeah, sure. 'Out of sorts.'"

"Anyway, we had a little fun in Hawaii. Apparently it meant more to me than to him." She shrugged, trying not to lose her composure. "No big deal."

"Oh, hun, of course it is. I can tell by looking at you. And I really think you're wrong. I know Kade. He's been in here for years mooning over you. A guy that is that infatuated just doesn't have a one-night stand with his brother's best friend. Especially someone like Kade."

She had thought so, but apparently she had been wrong. Very wrong. "Well, I haven't heard from him in months. So I am assuming that the infatuation is over."

He opened his mouth to argue, but she held up her hand. "No more. I don't have time. Could you get Chef to prepare some of that jambalaya to go for me? Enough for the three of them—which will be a lot. Those Seals are going to eat me out of house and home. Oh, and can you handle tomorrow night? I know it's a lot to ask, but I thought maybe I should stick around the house. I feel like Mal has something to tell me."

He wanted to say more. She could tell by the look in his eye, but apparently thought better of it. He left her alone, and she finished shutting down the computer. It would take a few moments to prepare herself to face off with Kade. And they would…have a face off.

But first, she wanted to know what made him look that way, and just why the hell he looked so sickly.

. . . . .

"Your sister's a looker," Chief said from the backseat.

Kade barely held back the growl that rumbled in his chest. He couldn't help it. Seeing her had brought about so many emotions that he still didn't have under control. The possessiveness hit him out of left field. And what right did he have to feel that way? Four months had passed. Even if he had reasons for staying away—good reasons—they didn't mean anything right now. She wasn't his, never would be.

Mal laughed. "Hey, watch yourself, Chief. There's a good chance she'd beat you with your injured arm."

"You're not going to warn me off her?" Chief asked.

"Naw, if she doesn't want you, she'll let you know. Right, Kade?"

He glanced at his best friend, trying to figure out if there was another meaning. He had been tossing out strange comments for over a month now. But every time he looked at Mal, he appeared relaxed and gave Kade no hint of any other meaning.

"Sure. After running a bar for a few years, Shannon can handle herself."

Chief sighed. "Not that I can do anything about it tonight. I'm so damned tired from the trip. Damn bones are creaking."

"That's because you're old, Chief," Mal said.

"You got that right," Chief replied. "Although something did smell good in the bar."

"If I know Shannon, she'll be bringing us something home to eat, and I am sure it will be jambalaya."

Kade would normally welcome a bowl, but he hadn't had much of an appetite since returning from their mission. He knew the commander, along with his doctors, were worried about it. Mal pulled up to Shannon's house and parallel parked in front of it. She had one of the historical homes in the Garden District with the iron work fence, the famous balconies, and a garden Kade's mother would definitely kill in two weeks. He had always loved the house, probably almost as much as Shannon did. It always felt like he was coming home when they visited.

"Wow, this is your sister's?"

Mal nodded. "Yeah. It was our grandmother's years ago. She sold it and moved north. Shannon bought it a few years ago after Katrina. She had to repair a little bit here and there, but it is looking pretty good."

They grabbed their gear, and Kade felt the familiar twinge of pain in his knee. After pulling in a few breaths, he followed Mal and Chief up the walkway and into the house. It was dark and panic settled in his chest. He thought after three months, he would be over this stupid fear. Now, though, he felt his heart hammering against his ribs and his throat was closing up.

Mal turned on the lights in the foyer and tossed him a glance. Checking on him again. Like he was some kind of damned invalid. He had never told Mal about his new problem—problems—but he knew his friend sensed it.

"Why don't you take the guest room down here? The stairs are going to be a bitch on your knee."

He nodded and headed off to the room. He needed a shower and a shot of whiskey. Or maybe two whiskeys. He pulled off his clothes with just a few twinges. When he was finally naked, Kade stood there, looking at himself in

37

the mirror. He was a fucking mess. The injuries were healing, but there were still times he was amazed he got through the day without losing it.

He glanced down at his knee and cringed. It was swollen again, but nothing that a little ice wouldn't fix. He didn't need to look at the marks on his back. Even though they had healed, he could still feel them as if he had just been injured. He probably always would.

He heard the front door open just as he stepped into the shower. The house was old, and the wood flooring made it easy to hear movements. He heard her approach the guest room, hesitate, then after a moment or two, she walked away. With a sigh that was half regret and half relief, he picked up the soap and the rag. The hot water pounded on his back, releasing some of the tension that had been keeping him on edge.

He could admit that he'd been worried about facing Shannon. He had avoided it for months, broke off any contact after the total fucked up mess their assignment became. He knew she deserved an explanation, but he'd taken the cowards way out and not called. Hell, he didn't even email her. And there was one thing that he hated being and that was a coward. He would have never thought it would happen to him. He'd taken life in the Seals as one of the greatest adventures. Now, though, he wasn't sure he'd ever be able to put his gear on again.

He closed his eyes, trying to stamp out the feelings that thought brought about, but it didn't help. Every time he did, images from the firefight, of watching one of his best friends get shot, feeling the bullet piercing his skin...

Fuck. People who thought that you didn't remember things like that were fucked in the head. They didn't seem to understand that people would live with the memories the rest of their lives. And fuck, he didn't need to go back there, didn't want to remember how screwed up everything had become and how all of them had come back with more than just a little baggage, including the coffin of one of their own.

He pushed aside the irritation and the damn fucking vulnerability that seemed to choke him constantly and finished his shower.

He might consider himself a coward in a lot of ways now, but it was definitely time to face Shannon.

Chapter Six

Shannon finished pouring the casserole into a pot to warm up when she heard footsteps behind her. She didn't have to turn around to see who it was. She knew it was Kade. Something stirred on the back of her neck anytime he was near.

"It should be warmed up in just a sec."

He hesitated for a second, then he stepped over the threshold. She didn't want to turn around until she was composed. She didn't want to cry, didn't want pity from a man who would probably disdain female tears. The only men who didn't complain about her tears were her gay friends.

When she had herself under control, she turned to face him.

"Do y'all know how long you're going to be in town?"

He studied her for a second. "We have a week off before we have to go back."

She nodded. "Why don't you have a seat at the kitchen table? I'll get some bread cut up."

Before she could do that, he said, "Shannon."

She knew that tone, knew that he was going to try and let her down easy. She wasn't in the mood. Her feelings were too near the surface, a bubbling caldron of irritation, pain and shock.

"Yes?"

"I thought you would want to talk about us."

His normally easy voice sounded strained, as if he

were barely holding onto his temper. Why was he mad at her?

"I got the impression there was no 'us.'"

Kade stared at her then with those deep blue eyes of his, as if trying to find out if she were telling the truth. Did he think she would beg him back into her bed? *Fat chance there, buddy.*

"I thought women liked to discuss these things."

"Maybe. Most of the time. But you made it pretty clear by not contacting me. I guess I could beg for a reason, but those are just made up most of the time, right? I mean, when you break up with someone, most of the time it's because they just weren't for you." She forced herself to shrug as if it were nothing big. "It's fine, Kade. You didn't have to pretend it was something it wasn't. I won't bother you."

He muttered something under his breath, and she got a bit of satisfaction over that.

Frustrated? Suck it up, Seal.

"Now, I'm going to get the jambalaya ready for y'all, and then I'm taking a long, hot shower. It's been a bitch of a day."

He stared at her as if she had grown another head.

"It wasn't that I didn't think it was special. It was. Just...things are different now."

She cocked her head to one side and studied him. "How so?"

She knew it was rude, but she didn't give a damn. If he wanted to drag all this shit out, then she wasn't going to make it easy on him.

"Just...things happened. I...," he swallowed, and his breathing increased. "I'm not fit for a relationship right now."

"Okay."

He frowned harder. "Okay?"

"Listen, Kade, I'm not sure what kind of women you

usually get involved with, but I'm a sister of a Seal. I know what your life is like. And I know that sometimes you come back a little less stable than before. Don't forget, Mal stays with me most of the time after he comes back from a long mission. The fact you don't want me hurts, of course. I am strong enough to say that."

"I didn't say I didn't want you."

The words seemed to be torn from some place deep inside of him.

"But..."

He swallowed again. "I just can't."

She sighed, regret and pain filling her heart. She wanted to yell, but couldn't. Not with him looking so damned sad, not to mention her other two houseguests.

"Tell you what, Seal. You get your shit together, then you can let me know. But I'm not waiting around forever."

Just then, her brother walked up behind him. "Is that jambalaya I smell?"

She smiled at the happiness in her brother's voice. He always said the smell of jambalaya simmering in the kitchen was the one thing that reminded him of home.

"Sure, and I have some bread too. But first, I have to get changed and de-stress." She walked to the doorway and had to inch past Kade. Dammit, the man wasn't making it easy on her. She could smell him, the soap he had used, and the wild untamed scent that was totally Kade. She inched past him, gave her brother a hug, and then walked to her bedroom.

As soon as she shut the door, she leaned back against it. Her heart was beating a mile a minute, her body a strange mixture of hurt and arousal. How could he still do that to her? Of course, she hadn't really accepted the end, not that there was actually a beginning. Still, there had been that kernel of hope she had held onto. She felt the sharp jab to the chest. Damn the man for getting her tangled up. She knew he still wanted her. Well, she was

pretty sure. But something was holding him back. Mal?
She figured if Mal knew about them, he wouldn't have
brought him here. He played the easygoing brother, but he
would kill a man for looking sideways at his sisters.

She closed her eyes and felt the tears slip free. She
couldn't do this. *Would* not do this. She had to hold herself
together. The three men in her house where all holding on
by a very tiny thread. Mal might not have talked to her
about it, but she knew the last mission was worse than any
of the ones they had been on.

Drawing in a deep breath, she started to undress. She
needed to get her emotions under control. They didn't need
a blabbering woman crying all over them.

By the time she had changed into comfy clothes and
splashed water on her face, her temper had cooled and she
had washed away some of the fatigue that was pulling her
down. She dried her face and looked at herself in the
mirror. She had always been considered the "healthy one."
Teenage years being Jocelyn Dupree's sister hadn't been
easy, that was for sure. With her tall, athletic body, Jocelyn
had always made Shannon feel like a goblin. But in her
late teens, she had grown into her body. She was full,
curvy, and she thought, happy with what God gave her.
Unlike some of her friends who dieted constantly, she
never lacked for male companionship. And she had always
thought Kade liked her just the way she was.

With a sigh, she decided to clean the rest of her
makeup off and get out there. Those Seals needed someone
who could hold it together.

And if there was one thing about the Dupree women,
they held it together with an iron fist.

. . . . .

"So, do you know if your sister is seeing someone?"

Deke asked Mal.

Again, Kade had to bite back a growl. Being in her house, being that close to her, had his possessiveness growing.

Mal looked at him then smiled at Deke. "Nope. Not that I know of. There was that one guy...Mike?"

"Jonathon," Kade said.

"Yeah, Mike was the guy before. Well, good old Jon was trying his best to tie her down. Shannon kicked him to the curb. I really thought he would be at the wedding in Hawaii."

"If she cooked this, I think I'm in love."

Mal laughed. "Oh, lord, no. You don't want Shannon's cooking."

"Am I being disparaged in my own kitchen?

He wasn't ready for her. Would he ever get used to being this close? He didn't think so. Before Hawaii, he could control his feelings more easily. Now, he seemed to be completely off. Nothing seemed to work. He felt powerless to do anything about it. Every day he was worried he would freak the hell out.

Before, she had been sexy. There wasn't anything she could wear that would make her look ugly. Shannon personified beauty. Now, though, she looked...cuddly. Due to the cold weather, she had pulled on soft, pink sweats. They shouldn't make her any more attractive, but they did. Just seeing her that way made his body respond. He wanted to do nothing more than pull her into his arms and snuggle. Then fuck her until neither of them remembered their names.

The thought had his brain almost shutting down. From the time he'd been medevac'd out, he had been out of it. Even thinking about Shannon hurt. He had thought that there was a good chance he couldn't be the man for her anymore. He knew he couldn't. Right now, he was desperately trying not to imagine her tied to his bed as he

44

pleasured her.

"Of course I'm making fun of your cooking. It sucks," Mal said, agreeable.

"No pancakes for you," she admonished, but she smiled when she said it.

"Okay, I take that back. Everything Shannon makes sucks, except for her pancakes."

Deke smiled at her. "Cooking isn't that important when a woman can look as beautiful as you do in a pair of sweats."

Shannon laughed and placed her hand on Deke's shoulder in a friendly gesture. Something rumbled in his chest at the sight. She glanced at him, her eyes widening a bit.

"I see y'all definitely left me nothing to eat."

"You don't eat this late," Mal said. "Does she, Kade?"

He was still irritated that her hand was on Chief's shoulder. The contact was far from intimate, but it was driving Kade insane.

"So she claims."

She glanced at him again, her brows now furrowed. But she said nothing to defy his suggestive tone.

"I ate something earlier, before you got here. I would have been home if you would have told me you were bringing guests."

"I had to drag these two along."

She shook her head and went to get herself some water. "What kind of Seal needs to be forced to come to New Orleans? You boys need to have your heads checked out."

"If I had known you would be waiting here, I would have offered to drive," Deke said.

She laughed. It was that sexy little flirty laugh he loved. And she was doing it for some guy. Some other guy, who was looking at her like he had a chance at her. Dammit, didn't Chief know not to take advantage of

45

Shannon? She was *his*.

He pulled back from that thought. She wasn't his. Never would be again.

Fuck, he needed some rest.

"I think I better get some sleep."

"Do you need anything?" Shannon asked. Her tone was normal, but there was a hint of something else there. He looked over at her, but he couldn't decide if it was wishful thinking.

"No, just some sleep. It was a long drive from Virginia."

She nodded in understanding.

"This old man needs some sleep if he's going to see any of New Orleans tomorrow. Been a while since I've been here," Deke said.

"If you need someone to show you around, let me know. I scheduled myself off the rest of the week to spend time with Mal. I'm sure he will get sick of me within six hours," Shannon said.

Deke smiled at her. "Thanks."

Kade and Deke made their way to their rooms. The guest room was right by the stairs, and Deke stopped him there.

"You don't have a problem if I ask Shannon out while I'm here, do you?"

He wanted to tell him to stay the hell away from Shannon. He wasn't her type. He was too old. And she was his.

But that wasn't true. None of it.

"No problem, mate."

He turned and walked into his room, thinking that for the first time in a week, he would be taking the hard meds.

. . . . .

46

"You want to tell me why you brought this motley crew to my house without warning?"

Mal shook his head. "I didn't want to say I was bringing them if I couldn't convince them. Both of them just wanted to spend the week sitting around their quarters. I thought it wasn't a good idea."

"That bad?"

He nodded. "Actually, probably worse. We lost Forrester."

The name brought to mind the young kid that had spent his honeymoon in New Orleans just a year earlier. "Oh, shit."

"Yeah, Amanda is kind of a wreck."

"I can imagine. How are you doing?"

"You can see that my beautiful face is just fine."

She took his hand and tugged on it. "No. I want to know if you are doing okay."

For once, Mal's expression turned serious. "Yeah. A few dreams here and there, but no depression. Seriously, I was knocked unconscious and missed the worst of it."

"I take it Deke and Kade didn't? They looked a little roughed up."

"They look amazing compared to what they looked like a few weeks ago. Kade especially. I understand we almost lost him. He was trying to save Forrester."

Her heart jumped into her throat. "Do Kade's folks know?"

"Probably not. He's shut down. He was quiet before, but now he's damned creepy."

"Mal," she admonished. "That's no way to talk about your best friend."

"Yeah, I know. But it's the truth. You saw. He barely talks now. It's like he's not there. I thought you might be able to help out."

She studied her brother's eyes. "Like how?"

"He's always had a crush on you. You have to know

47

that."

"Yes."

"Well, he always seems so...relaxed around you. He talks to you more than he talks to any woman I've seen him with."

She dropped his hands. "So you want to act as my pimp?"

He rolled his eyes. "Good God, no. I might have to bleach my brain to get that image out of there."

"Why don't you explain what you want from me, Mal?"

"He talks to you. If you could get him to listen, to come back to life, that would be fantastic."

"So a miracle?"

He chuckled. "No, just a sounding board. Not sure if it will work, but I thought maybe you would bring him out of his shell."

"I'll try."

"That's all I ask, sis." He leaned forward and gave her a kiss. "I'm going to go to bed. You need help with the dishes?"

Normally, she would force him to do all the cleaning up. Looking at him though, she saw the dark circles under his eyes and the fatigue weighing him down. He was worried about his friends, and the stress of that and the drive was probably enough to blank any man out, even a Seal.

"Naw, I got it."

She went through the motions as she listened to him walk up the stairs. She couldn't let him see just how much that affected her. He knew it hurt for her to hear, but she also knew her brother. He was worried. Very worried. Kade was usually so self-contained, but now that Mal pointed it out, she realized he was right. Kade had shut down. She rinsed off the dishes and put them in her dishwasher as she thought of his behavior.

He had always been quiet, just as Mal had said, but dammit, he had always been...well, like a guy hiding a secret. A fun secret. His eyes had always sparkled, and he had always been willing to listen and join in when asked. Now, it was as if he saw himself as separate from the world. Even from his closest friend.

She started the washer then began cleaning off the table. Was it as simple as guilt? He hadn't saved Forrester. He had survived. Maybe that was why he was holding back from her, and even Mal?

Did she want to take a chance on helping him? Getting him to talk, trying to draw him out, would hurt. Hurt a lot, that was for sure. Being in the same house as him had her aching from the inside out. Hell, just hearing that funky noise he'd made when she'd touched Deke had sent ribbons of lust streaming through her blood.

She paused and straightened.

He had been cool, at least he'd looked that way. But, in his eyes...her breath caught. "He's jealous."

For a second she thought back, tried to debunk the idea. Why would he be jealous of a simple pat? She understood maybe getting upset if she had slept with Deke, but this was nothing. It had to be that he still had feelings for her, yes? Why else would he have growled?

That had her looking at the situation in a different manner. Did she want to put herself out there, take a chance on being hurt again?

Maybe.

Worse, did she want to take the chance of losing him forever? If he felt guilt for what happened, did he think he wasn't good enough for her? That would make sense. She could at least put out feelers, push him a little. Knowing Mal, he'd been handling his friend with kid gloves. While her brother was a kickass Seal, just like every other Dupree man, he had a gooey, soft center. He hated to see someone he loved hurt and would do anything to protect him or her.

She sat in the chair with a thunk. Well, damn. She had to look at the situation a little differently now. He might be a little rough around the edges now, and she was still pissed at him, but he needed her. He needed more than just a friend, if her suspicions were right.

She would just push some buttons on that damned hardheaded Seal tomorrow and see what happened.

If there was anything worth the pain, it was Francis McKade. And if he was too stupid to realize she was good for him, she'd smack him upside the head and walk away.

She had to try because she didn't want to spend the rest of her life regretting it.

Chapter Seven

Kade opened his eyes to the blinding sun. It felt as if someone had poured acid on them. He slammed his lids shut with a groan. He had been so tired the night before that he'd forgotten to shut the blinds. No wonder he was burning up.

"Fuck," he said.

"Is that any way to talk in my house?"

He was slow to react the moment he heard her voice. He was barely awake, dealing with a blinding pain in his head, and the woman of his dreams was in his room. Her slow, New Orleans accent was threaded with amusement and low enough to send heat racing through his blood. Damn, he was naked but for the sheet over him.

Slowly, he opened his eyes and glanced to the doorway. Damn, the woman was gorgeous. Shit, he didn't need this. He was still dealing with being in her house, being within feet of her, and now she was standing there smiling at him. She was leaning against the doorjamb, a steaming mug of coffee in her hand, and she was wearing some kind of flimsy robe with red flowers all over it.

Of course, without little provocation, his cock went completely hard. What man wouldn't react like that to seeing her there? Her curls were dripping over shoulders, and her face was scrubbed free of makeup. Dammit, he wanted to see her like that every morning. Wanted her in his bed, wanted to wake up beside her, snuggle against her, then love her slowly awake. And that was why he hadn't wanted to come. He knew every minute—every second—of the day he was in New Orleans, his need to touch her would grow. He knew it would be impossible to resist her. Less than twelve hours and he was ready to beg her. Mentally, he chastised himself. He couldn't take her to bed like he wanted, to love her until neither of them knew their names. The man he was in Hawaii had that right. He didn't now, and he couldn't stand hurting her again.

"I'm sure you've heard worse than that with your brothers around."

She smiled as she took a sip. God was not smiling on him, he knew it then and there because she walked into the room. She closed the blinds then leaned against the dresser.

"Do you have any plans today?"

He knew she asked a question, but he couldn't seem to answer. His brain was melting. *Holy fuck.* The robe she was wearing hit her mid-thigh. If she moved just the wrong way, he would find out if she had any panties on. Jesus, what the hell did he ever do to God to deserve this?

"Kade?"

He shook his head, trying to break free of that mesmerizing bit of leg she was showing him and looked up at her face. Those eyes were studying him, and he felt himself shiver. He didn't physically do it, but everything in him trembled as he tried to hold onto his control.

"Not sure."

She took another sip and shifted her weight. Dammit. He couldn't decide if he wanted her to leave or stay. Either one would be bad and good.

"Do you want to come with Deke and me?"

He wanted to. He really wanted to. The idea that Chief was sniffing around her didn't sit well with him. The man had a reputation with women. He might be older than most of the other Seals, but he tended to have more women, if rumors were correct. But even at his age, he didn't seem to be settling down. The last woman Kade had seen him with was younger than Shannon.

Still, Kade knew it wouldn't be a good idea to tag along. He could handle her in small doses, but he needed a break every now and then. And there was a good chance that he might beat the hell out of Chief if he got too handsy.

"Naw. I thought I would hang around the house today."

She frowned. "Your leg's not bothering you, is it?"

"Did Mal tell you I hurt it?"

"No. You were favoring it last night."

He nodded. "It's stiff from the drive. I thought I would take a hot bath, then put it up with some ice."

"Well, if you change your mind, we are leaving at eleven hundred."

He smiled. "Yes ma'am."

She patted him on his leg, and his eyes almost crossed. Just that simple touch had his body heating, his cock jumping. Damn, if the woman wasn't going to have him dead from lack of blood to his brain.

"There are some fresh pastries in the kitchen, and Mal is brewing some coffee."

She left, and he dropped his head back on the pillow. The scent of her was still in the room, and he probably would never smell that spicy perfume again without getting aroused. He knew she was still hoping for something, and dammit, he wanted to give it to her. But he couldn't trust himself. Not with his issues, or with her.

With a grimace, he sat up and stood. He hobbled, ignoring the pain shooting through his leg and the cock stand she had left him with.

. . . . .

"Do you want to tell me what's going on between you and Kade?" Deke asked.

Shannon choked on the sip of water she had just taken. She coughed a few times before gaining control.

"Sorry. I'm sometimes a little too blunt for my own good."

She shook her head and patted her lips with her napkin.

"No, really, I grew up with a lot of men in the house. One of them is Mal, who is not much different than you."

She took another sip of water and wiped away a couple of tears.

"Are you going to answer the question?" he asked just as bluntly as before.

She couldn't help but smile. From her experience, military men were always much more tenacious than other men. "Why do you ask?"

He rolled his eyes and took a bite of his sandwich. "He didn't look too happy when we left, and well, I feel like I'm poaching on his goods. We have a good working relationship, and I don't want this to get in the way."

She raised one eyebrow. "Poaching on his goods? I'm not sure I like that phrase."

"Beg your pardon, but I didn't ask."

She threw her head back and laughed. From the moment they had left her house, she had been delighted by Deke. If she wasn't in love with the surly idiot she'd left behind, she definitely would be interested in him.

"That's a pretty sound," he said, his gaze resting on her lips.

"Why thank you."

"So, quit screwing around and trying to avoid the question."

"I'm not sure what we are."

He nodded. "I had a feeling." He sighed. "Well, I was hoping that there would be a chance. I knew he was all moony-eyed over some woman when he returned from that wedding."

She set her elbow on the table then settled her chin on her hand. "I have a feeling you don't really want a chance. And it has nothing to do with me being Mal's sister or the fact that I am somewhat involved with the other idiot my brother brought home. Sure, you'd flirt with me, have a little romance, even take me to bed. But I have a feeling that you'd be out the door and I would be out of your mind before your next mission."

His lips twitched. "Well, why do you think that is, Ms. Dupree?"

"I do love a Georgia accent, Mr. Berg." She took a sip of water. "Well, I think you're carrying a torch for someone."

He looked stunned and blinked at her, those ridiculously long eyelashes catching her attention. It was really a shame both of them were tangled up with someone else. He was a delicious man to look at.

His cheeks turned ruddy and she couldn't believe he was blushing. He cleared his throat. "That's not true."

"Aha, I'm right. You've been here before, yes?"

He nodded. "On my honeymoon."

Her heart did that little dance it did at the romance of it. "So walking around here with me has really bugged you, hasn't it?"

He made a face, and she laughed.

"You still have the hots for your ex?"

He sighed. "God, don't tell her that. We can't be together."

Shannon heard the longing in his voice, and her heart did that little jig again. Who would have thought that the Viking was such a romantic?

"Is she married again?"

"No."

"Had the change?" she asked.

"What?"

"You know, decided she was really a man instead of a woman?"

"Good God, no." He shook his head. "And I thought Mal was bad."

"She's not in jail, I am assuming. What's stopping you, Seal?"

"Just one of those things."

She shook her head. "It isn't 'just one of those things.' Not if walking around here brought your honeymoon back to you. You still want her. I thought Seals had more balls than to sit around and say that it isn't good?"

"We're not good together."

She frowned. "The sex is bad?"

"Lord in heaven, you have a mouth on you."

She laughed again, delighted she'd made him blush. God, was there anything sweeter than a hardened military man who was still in love with his ex-wife? She didn't think so.

"What I mean is we are...combustible. But not just in the bedroom."

"Ah, the temperament. Comes with the passion."

"If I had known I was going to face the inquisition while we were out, I would have made sure to not take the pain pill."

"I guess Mal didn't tell you about me."

"Other than you were single, could handle yourself, and well, that you're pretty."

She narrowed her eyes. "You added that last one in."

He smiled. "Okay, I did."

"I guess Mal didn't tell you the nickname my brothers gave me, did he?"

He shook his head.

"I was known as the informer."

He waited for a second, and when she didn't continue, he asked, "The informer?"

"Yes. We had a big family: four boys, two girls, and a

56

mother who worked by my father's side to get the business going. When my mother worried about the boys, she always let me go with them. And if I didn't, she made sure I got to question them. I can get an answer out of anyone."

"Is that why Mal let you go with me alone?"

She snorted. "First of all, Mal doesn't let me do anything. I stopped answering to a man the day I turned eighteen. Secondly, I don't think so. See, knowing my brother, he's going to go catting around after a few of his lost loves. He's not ready to settle down yet, so I know he will go to the women he knows won't get clingy."

Deke rolled his eyes. "Talk about someone who's carrying a torch."

She zeroed in on that statement. "Do tell."

Deke's eyes widened almost comically. "No. No way. I am not ratting out an officer to his sister. I'll never live it down."

"Spoilsport."

"I would rather be called that than whatever the team would invent to pay me back for telling you something."

"Why don't we go do a little more walking? I need to stop by my bar. I just need to make sure there aren't any problems."

"I think I can handle that."

She nodded. "And maybe we'll stop at a voodoo store, and I'll buy something to make you talk."

"Don't even think about it. I have a healthy respect for that shit."

Laughing, she patted his hand.

"If Kade screws this up with you, I want first dibs at a date."

Amused with him, with the solemn expression on his face, she smiled.

"You're the first man I'd call."

. . . . .

57

"So, how long you in town for?"

Mal smiled at Verna, and Kade tried not to cuss. He really hadn't wanted to come to the bar, but Mal had insisted, telling him he needed to get out of the house. He knew his friend was right, but it didn't mean he wanted to sit there with the skanky woman wrapped around Mal like he was a life preserver on the Titanic. And he didn't want to be in Shannon's bar.

"We only have a week of leave. So not long. Just needed to get out of Virginia, and I wanted to check on my sister. Has she been seeing anyone?"

Verna shook her head. "That new restaurant owner from down the street has been sniffing around. He's one of the Augustins. But she shut him down. She told me he was just trying to scope out the competition."

"Are we talking about Beau? He has always had a thing for her. When we were in high school, he used to follow her around like she was the goddess of New Orleans."

Verna laughed, and Kade took another quick drink of his water. The woman's laugh was equal to nails on a chalkboard to him.

"I could see that. She said it wasn't that, but man he moons over her. Well, speak of the devil."

He followed the waitress's line of vision, and his heart did that little skip. The bright yellow dress she wore was made of some kind of flimsy fabric that clung to her generous curves. It dipped low between her breasts and stopped just above her knee. She was laughing at something Deke said, and dammit, he couldn't help the way the air backed up in his lungs.

"Looks like they had a good time," Mal said.

Indeed it did. Her face glowed with happiness as she looked up at Deke. He leaned closer and said something to her. She laughed, and although it wasn't loud, he could hear it. It wrapped around his heart and gave a little tug.

She was out having the time of her life with one of his buddies. Meanwhile, he had been stuck with Mal and the waitress from hell. He was drinking the damned water because the lazy woman had yet to get him another beer. She spotted them, and he felt her attention stay on him a moment or two longer than it had on Mal. They walked over to the table.

"I had a feeling y'all would be out. Did you do anything more interesting than entertain Verna?" Shannon asked.

"There isn't anything more interesting than that," Mal said, sending the waitress into peals of laughter.

"Verna, you need to get back to work. I have a feeling that both of these Seals need another beer."

She made a face, but she did it all the same.

Shannon settled in the chair next to her brother. Chief took the chair next to her and acted as if he had a right to sit there. Between them. He shot a look at Kade, but then turned his attention to Shannon.

"Really, Mal, the woman is an idiot," Shannon said.

"Why do you keep her around, then?" Mal asked as he scooped up another handful of snack mix.

"When you aren't around, she's a pretty good waitress, and I don't have the patience to train someone else right now. She might not be the brightest bulb, but at least I don't have to work with her anymore."

"She's not stupid," Mal said.

"She went and got a two-for-one tattoo and was amazed that they spelled her name wrong on one of them. Really, who has their name tattooed on their own ass? I'll tell you, an idiot."

Deke chuckled. "It isn't like you couldn't find another woman in this town. It's filled with them."

"Yeah, Deke had a couple of women practically slobbering on him at the voodoo shop. It was embarrassing. I thought they might use a love potion on him."

She leaned back in her chair, and Deke put his arm over the back of it. Like they were a couple. *Fuck*. He told himself for the millionth time that he didn't have a right to get mad, but dammit, Deke wasn't her boyfriend. He wasn't anything to her.

"So, I was trying to talk him into a night on Bourbon Street, but he claims he's an old, tired man," Shannon said.

"I said I would enjoy a nice, relaxing dinner with you. Not some loud bar with a bunch of tourists," Deke said.

His flirtatious tone had Kade grinding his teeth. He read the signs. Chief had shifted his chair closer, leaned into her, as if they were on a date. As if he had a right to touch her. Kade felt his temper rising, but he fought it. He was pretty sure Shannon wouldn't be happy if he embarrassed her by re-breaking Chief's arm.

"What's on the agenda tomorrow?" she asked.

"I plan to follow you around like a puppy dog," Chief said.

Her eyebrows rose slightly, but she didn't say anything. If the red haze of anger and jealousy hadn't blinded him, he would have noticed that she was surprised by Chief's behavior. It was lost on him. All he saw was his friend coming onto the woman he had been in love with for too long. He did the only thing a Seal could do—other than shoot Chief.

Kade stood and walked around the table. Without a word, he grabbed Shannon by the arm and hauled her up.

"That's enough of that," he said.

Kade said nothing else as he dragged her out of the bar. She complained all the way, calling him many names in English and Creole. Some he knew, and he was pretty sure he didn't want to know the others. When they reached the street, he scanned it for her convertible and found it easily. He started to drag her along to it, but she dug in her heels and forced him to stop.

"What in holy hell are you doing?" she asked, loud enough that people passing took notice.

He turned to face her and couldn't think. Right now, he was so damned aroused and irritated, his brain just would not form words. Besides, she was a sight to behold when she was angry. Her face was flushed. Her green eyes were spitting daggers at him, and dammit, she was breathing heavily. With each breath she took, the delicate flesh rose about the flimsy neckline of her dress.

"You do not drag me out of a bar like you own me. I am not into he-men who think they can order me around. Just who the hell do you think you are?"

The darker side he wanted to control came slithering to the top and lashed out at her. He cupped the back of her neck and pulled her to him. He attacked her mouth then, letting all his frustration, his needs, his desires wash over her, over both of them. She resisted at first, but it was futile. He knew she wanted him. He used it to entice her, slipping his tongue between her lips and tasting her.

By the time he pulled back, they were both breathing unsteadily.

"You choose, now. You come back to your place with me, or you tell me to fuck off."

He watched her lashes lower as she sighed. It sounded like regret, and he realized he might have made a big mistake with her. Maybe he had pushed his luck with her, and she had written him off. She wasn't a woman who had to wait around for a man, especially one that had been a jackass.

But in the next instant, she looked up at him, her gaze direct, unwavering. He felt as if she were looking into his soul.

"Let's go."

Chapter Eight

Shannon's nerves were popping with excitement and a little bit of fear by the time she walked into her house. The ride home had been quiet, Kade not saying a word. She didn't live far from her business, but it had seemed to take forever to make it back to her house. Kade shut the door behind him, and she set her purse and keys on the table in the front hallway and faced him.

He looked so different. Fire flamed in his eyes, darkening them with the desire he felt for her. "Last chance, Dupree."

The way he said it sounded scary and thrilling at the same time. She knew he was trying to give her an out. He hadn't spoken of any commitment. At the moment, he wasn't thinking of the future—she was sure of that. Doing this, she was taking a chance on her heart but not her body. Even in his state, she knew that he would never abuse her. He couldn't think beyond today. She understood that. It was the only way he could cope with whatever he was going through. Still, she knew that he would never dally with her if he hadn't felt some kind of connection. She knew he was good, a really good man. And right now, he needed her.

"I don't need any warnings, McKade." She settled her hands on her hips and lifted her chin. He wasn't going to scare her off, not now. "Unless you aren't up to the task, Seal."

He hesitated for a second, as if not believing she had

62

just challenged him. The silence stretched as they stood there staring at each other. For a moment, just a moment, she thought he might walk away. That scared her more than his mood right now. Then, he grabbed her arm again and dragged her back to her room. Not that she was fighting him at all. She wanted this, wanted him in her bed.

He shut the French doors behind him and locked them. When he turned to her, she felt the first little lick of real fear. He masked his emotions, and she couldn't tell what he was thinking. Shannon knew he was a good man, but she wondered at the moment if he realized it himself.

"Strip."

She hesitated, not sure if she heard him right. This was not the playful lover she knew in Hawaii, the one who laughed with her in bed. This man was definitely dangerous. While he did scare her a bit, there was another emotion coursing along with it. *Arousal.*

"Did you hear me, Shannon? Do it now, or I'll punish you."

She shivered at the thought of what he might do. It would definitely be more than last time, she was sure of that. She did as he ordered but slowly. She wanted to make sure that he understood she was giving this to him. It was her choice, not his.

She removed her high-heeled sandals, kicking them to the wall and out of the way. Then, she slowly pulled down the zipper to her dress. She shimmied out of it, letting it fall to the floor. He showed no emotion in his expression. If anything, he looked mad. His lips turned down in a concentrated frown. His eyes, though, told another story. Heat was burning still, even hotter than before.

"Panties and bra too, Shannon."

He didn't raise his voice, but she heard the command. His tone was low and gravelly. It did odd things to her. She liked a little playing in the bedroom, but she had never seen herself as someone who would be into hardcore

BDSM. But that low, demanding voice was starting to get to her. In fact, it made her want to make him happy, to please him.

She undid her bra, and he watched. A first for her. She had never stripped for a man. Not that she hadn't thought about it, or didn't have enough confidence in herself to do it. She had just never wanted to do it for a man. Until now.

She shook her shoulders, freeing the fabric and causing her breasts to sway slightly. The cool air hit her nipples, and she drew in a sharp breath. They were already so sensitive. She could not imagine what it would feel like when he touched them. By the time she got it free, she thought he made a sound, but she wasn't sure. He still showed no emotion on his face, and if she hadn't been so tuned in to him, she probably would have missed it.

She held the bra out and then dropped it to the floor. She waited.

"The panties."

Again, not loud, but even more demanding. Shannon got the feeling that Kade was barely holding onto his control, and something in her wanted to push him over the edge. She turned to face the bed, giving him full view of the red thong she wore. Again, as slowly as she could, she skimmed them down her legs, bending over as she did so. Her pussy throbbed, her body ready to be touched, pleasured. She stepped out of them.

"Turn around."

She did, and the man she faced scared her a little bit. She could see the way he was grinding his teeth. His jaw flexed each time he did. And his eyes...they were as dark and dangerous as the man who stood before her.

"Get on the bed, on your back, and spread your legs."

She wanted to tell him not to order her around. A little play was one thing, but being ordered about was different. Everything in her independent nature wanted to rebel. But something deeper, something that yearned to be with

64

Kade, was stronger. It aroused her on some level she had never touched before. Her need spiked. She did as he ordered and waited. Cool air washed over her pussy as she felt it dampen. God, he hadn't even touched her, and she was dripping wet.

He approached the bed, still fully dressed. His blue gaze travelled down her body, and she felt it as if he were touching her. There was no doubt of the bulge in his pants. He was definitely aroused. He apparently wasn't getting rid of his clothes anytime soon. *Dammit.*

He skimmed his hand up the inside of her thigh. Those callused fingers danced over her sensitive skin. She couldn't help the shiver that moved through her body.

"I need a word that tells me I've pushed you too far. Something easy to remember."

"Jazz."

"Do you understand what we are about to do? From this point on, I am in charge. I am the person in control of your pleasure."

She nodded then sucked in a breath as he began to finger her labia. That first little touch had flashes of heat sparking through her blood. It was such a simple touch. It shouldn't have her this close to the edge.

"Rules. No speaking unless I give you permission. Do you understand?"

"Yes."

As if to reward her, he pressed his thumb against her clit, and she almost lost it. She closed her eyes and hummed. God, the pressure pushed her closer, but before she could lift her hips, he slipped his thumb away. She opened her eyes.

"Oh, no, Shannon. You don't come unless I give it to you. I'll make you pay for that little stunt."

She opened her mouth to say she hadn't been that bad when he slapped her pussy. It wasn't hard, just a pat really, but she was already sensitive there, and pleasure rippled out over her.

"I didn't give you permission to speak." He settled on the bed next to her, shaking his head. "You really don't understand yet. Maybe you aren't ready for it."

As he spoke, he skimmed his fingers over her belly up to her breasts. He pinched her nipples. The action had her moaning and closing her eyes again. The man had the most talented fingers.

"Sadly, I can't turn back now, don't want to. It's been a long four months."

He slipped his hand up her neck and then placed his fingers against her mouth.

"Open up, baby."

She opened her eyes again and did as he ordered. He slid his index finger into her mouth. She could taste her arousal. Wanting to be naughty, she slipped her tongue over his finger. He sighed in appreciation then pulled his finger out of her mouth.

Without a word, he stood and pulled off his shirt. She didn't move, didn't want to break the spell he was casting on her.

Holy mother of God. With each inch of flesh he revealed, she became more entranced. Was there a chance he had gotten even more gorgeous? He had lost weight, which emphasized his sculpted physique. She wanted nothing more than to explore that body, but she lay on the bed, waiting for his command. That thrilled her more than the idea of touching him.

There was something wrong with her.

He unzipped his jeans and slipped them off. Of course, he wasn't wearing any underwear. If she had even thought about him walking around commando, she would have probably not been able to concentrate enough to talk. He shucked them off and stood before her, his hand on his cock, stroking it. He had his gaze locked on hers, daring her to watch. She couldn't resist. Watching his hand moving over his hardened cock, seeing the little pearl of pre-come easing out, had her yearning.

As if reading her thoughts, he asked, "Want a little taste, Shannon?"

There was a thread of amusement in his tone. And for a quick moment, he looked lighter than he had since he'd appeared in her bar.

She nodded. He inched closer to the bed. "Up on your knees."

Her eagerness to please had her moving as fast as possible. He pressed his cock against her mouth, and she gladly took him in. With shallow movements, he thrust in and out of her mouth. Just like in Hawaii, the taste of him had her lust surging. She wanted more, wanted him deep within her mouth, to feel him bump against the back of her throat. He did not allow it.

Instead, he continued, giving her just a small taste of him as he slid his hand down her back to her ass. He skimmed the separation between her cheeks and fingered her anus. She hummed against his cock, and he jolted, shoving his penis further into her mouth.

"You like that, huh?"

She figured it was rhetorical and didn't answer him.

"I have a feeling you would like some anal play, but not tonight."

He continued to tease her as he fucked her face, increasing the depth of his thrusts. Soon though, she could tell he was losing control. His movements were not that controlled, and when she slipped her tongue over the tip of his cock, he pulled away with a groan.

"Oh, that was bad, Shannon. Really, bad." He turned from her then, and she was left on her hands and knees, her body needing to be touched. Hell, she needed to touch him, to skim her hands over all that wonderful flesh.

Without turning around, he asked, "Do you have any scarves?"

67

"Yes, in the top right-hand drawer of the dresser."

He retrieved a couple of scarves and set them on the top of the dresser. Kade turned and smiled at her. It wasn't a huge smile, like the ones she was used to, but it was something. Even as frustrated as she was, it made her heart happy to see it.

"Come on," he said, offering her a hand for support. "Up, off the bed."

She did as ordered, excited to see what he would come up with next. Kade positioned her in front of the mirror.

"Look at you," he said, his voice deepening, and his accent thickening. She did as ordered and was struck by the image of them together. Her light brown skin against his lighter, tanned flesh. He stepped closer, his cock against her ass. He placed his hand against her stomach. She was so tuned in to his touch that the simple gesture had her body reacting. It was hard not to as he moved his hand up to her breasts, caressing the underside of them. Frustration built.

"I can tell from your face that you're not happy with me."

It wasn't a question, so she didn't respond. It was hard to even think at the moment. With each delicate touch, he had her blood pressure rising, her body becoming more and more in tune with him. He slipped his hand down to her pussy. Using his index finger, he traced her labia. She was dripping wet, slick with her desire, but he didn't say anything about that.

"Watch my hand."

She was already doing that, but she understood he wanted to see her expression. He dipped his finger into her pussy, and she sighed.

"What a pretty sound." He was still in control, but she heard the heat simmering in his voice.

As soon as he said it, she pulled her bottom lip between her teeth.

"Don't worry about showing your pleasure. The sweetest sound is hearing you moan my name."

He teased her for just a few more seconds before he pulled away. He took the first of the scarves, a red one with black designs on it, and slid it over her breasts. Her skin was so sensitive to his touch that it almost hurt as the delicate fabric slithered over her nipples. Kade's gaze was glued to the scarf as he moved it over her, his lips curving in satisfaction as she shivered.

He stepped beside her and slipped his finger under her chin and turned her face to him. Bending his head, he gave her a kiss, a soft brush of the lips. It had everything in her yearning for so much more.

When he pulled away, he said, "Spread your legs a little more, then place your hands on the dresser."

She did as ordered, and he slid the scarf between her legs. The slither of silky material against her sex almost sent her over the edge. It was barely a touch. He pulled the material tight against her.

Oh, God. She was going to come. He moved the scarf back and forth slightly as he nuzzled her neck. His cock was hard against her hip, and she knew he wanted her. But he was controlling himself, controlling her. She wasn't an innocent by any standards, but this was beyond what she had ever tried. He tightened the scarf more, the material separating her pussy lips.

She moaned as it rubbed against her clit, pressing ever so slightly but not enough to give her relief. He only gave her so much before he was tugging the scarf away and pulling her to the bed.

"On the bed," he ordered. He had seemed under control, but the deepening of his voice told her more. He was close to the edge, too.

Kade grabbed the second scarf. "Hands over your head."

She complied without thinking. She wanted him to

69

touch her again, wanted his hands on her. He wrapped it around her wrists then threaded it through her iron headboard. After completing the task, he stopped and looked down at her. His gaze slipped down her body, and she felt as if he was touching her everywhere.

In the next instant, he scowled. "Dammit. Condoms."

She smiled. "Bedside table drawer."

If anything, his expression turned darker.

"Oh, good lord, I had to talk."

"It's not that. It's the fact that you had condoms ready. Been seeing someone?"

She rolled her eyes. "They're the ones from Hawaii."

He didn't say anything as he pulled open the drawer. After grabbing one, he ripped open the package and then joined her on the bed. He set the opened package beside him. Then he settled between her legs and leaned down to give her pussy one long lick.

He smiled up at her. "Remember, don't come unless I give you permission."

He drove her crazy. He slipped his hands beneath her rear end and lifted her to his mouth. Then he attacked her. Over and over, he thrust his tongue into her pussy. When he took her clit into his mouth, he hummed against the bundle of nerves.

Damn. The tension that had been simmering now shot to her pussy. She wanted to move, wanted to slip her fingers through that blonde hair and thrust up against his mouth. He held her there, not allowing her any purchase.

Soon, though, he set her down, grabbed the condom. He rolled it on as fast as humanly possible, in her opinion. He lifted her up off the bed again and entered into her in one hard thrust. Without hesitating, he started moving. Each thrust was slow but deep, but not enough to please her. The way she was bound and the way he held her, she could do nothing but allow him to set the pace. Soon his movements were not so measured. He increased his rhythm.

"It's time, baby. Come for me."

He thrust into her hard as he pressed against her clit. She did as he ordered, bowing up against him and screaming out his name. She was still shuddering from her release as he started moving again, squeezing that tiny bundle of nerves between his fingers. She came again, bucking against him. He followed her as she crested again a few seconds later.

A short time later, he rolled off her and reached up to untie her wrists. "You feeling okay?" he asked.

She smiled at him, cupping his cheek. "Okay doesn't describe it."

He smiled, that old crooked smile she knew so well, and her breath caught. In the day he had been back, Kade had been distant and hadn't shown her the boyish grin she was used to.

"What?" he asked, as it started to slip away.

"Nothing. Just, you look good in my bed."

"So do you. How about a little snack?"

Keep it light, Dupree.

"Sure." She started to get out of bed, but he stayed her with his hand.

"No. You stay, I'll find something."

She nodded and watched as he pulled on his jeans. "I'll be right back."

She held her smile until she was alone. She sat up, pulled her knees to her chest and wrapped her arms around her legs. How sad was it that she was so excited to see him smile at her? Sad for both of them. Something was bad. Something had pushed him to his limit while they were gone. He was a strong man, but everyone had their breaking point.

All she could do was support him, let him know she was there for him.

And love him until he left at the end of the week.

71

Chapter Nine

Shannon settled against the pillows with a sigh that made Kade happier than he thought possible.

"That was a good idea. I didn't realize what an appetite I'd worked up."

He chuckled. "Really? I would have thought you needed a side of beef after that."

"Have you always been into BDSM? I've just never heard you talk about it."

"Does it bother you?"

She shook her head. "I wouldn't have let you touch me like that if I didn't want to. I like sex, but not enough to do something like that if I had issues with it."

He should have known that would be her answer. He had never met a woman so confident and straight up about her sexuality.

"I've always had some interest in it. But it's a little different now."

He could tell by her expression she wanted to ask him more. He was a little surprised by the need to control her. It almost overwhelmed his good senses. Kade just hoped he held himself in check for the week.

"Hm, I need a good night's sleep," she said. The patter of rain hit against the window, and Shannon was snuggled up against Kade as he pulled the sheet up. It was an image he had often dreamed of before his last mission.

He cleared his throat. "You're not the only one."

"And that rain is perfect. It always makes me so

72

drowsy. I love the sound of it."

She was already drifting into sleep. A selfish part of him wanted to stop her, keep her awake. They weren't going to have much time together. Kade wanted to savor every minute, try and draw out his visit.

There was a very good chance he was really screwing up. He had prepared himself to resist her, resist the crazy pull she always had on him. He had thought he could do it.

Inwardly, he snorted. Yeah, he could resist her. He'd been in New Orleans for less than forty-eight hours, and he had already crumbled.

"You're thinking too much."

Her breath tickled his chest. "What?"

She lifted her head and looked up at him. "You're thinking too much. Right now, your head is turning over all the things you're worried about."

"Yeah?"

She nodded. "Don't worry about it. Let it go."

"Aren't women supposed to get all talkative after sex?"

"If you don't do it right. Apparently, you haven't been doing it right."

Her sassy tone made him chuckle. How could he stay out of her bed? The woman had just submitted to him, and now she was messing with him. If a man could resist her, he had to be stupid or gay.

"Or maybe I had the wrong partners."

"I have to agree with that. Listen, I know you've got a lot on your plate. There is no pressure here, not right now. Let's just take it one day at a time. If you can handle that, Seal?"

Her tone was flirtatious, but there was a hint of steel beneath it. He had been preparing for a long, drawn out discussion of why he hadn't contacted her. Instead, she offered him nothing but understanding.

"I am more than up to the task."

"Good." She leaned up and gave him a kiss on the nose

then on his mouth. She lingered there, giving him a taste of her, tempting him. She pulled back, a smile curving her lips. In the soft moonlight, there in her room with the rain hitting the window, he knew he was still in love with her. His heart lurched at the thought, but he brushed the worry aside. One day at a time was what she wanted. That was what he would give her.

"You get some sleep," he said, trying to keep a lid on his emotions.

"You betcha." She chuckled, then settled back down and snuggled close to him.

He wanted this, wanted it more than he had ever wanted to be a Seal. It scared him a bit to know that. From the time he entered the Navy, he had wanted to be a Seal. He had questioned that in the last few months, but other than trying to protect her, he had never thought of giving up on Shannon.

Again, he shoved the thoughts aside and decided to do as ordered. A good night's sleep was what he really needed to get his head back on straight.

· · · · ·

Kade came awake with a shout. His heart was beating out of control, his body slick with sweat. He had been having these nightmares since he got back, but they hadn't been quite this bad. This one had been vivid, almost real to him.

Each time, he saw Forrester's face as he was shot, as the life seeped from him.

With a shake of his head, Kade stood and stretched. Shannon grumbled and settled deeper into the pillows. He brushed her hair from her face and noticed his hand was shaking. He wanted to touch her, to love her again, but he was too raw to handle that now. He needed to get his head

74

out of the dream and back onto the day. He went into the bathroom and splashed his face with some cool water, then found his jeans and pulled them on. Even through the closed blinds, he could see the first stirrings of the sunrise. There was one thing about a good bout of healthy sex. He had finally slept through the night. When he unlocked the door, he heard someone moving around in the kitchen. He had a feeling it was Mal. He didn't want to really deal with his friend without some coffee. Unfortunately, the coffee was, of course, in the kitchen. He could smell it brewing.

Kade squared his shoulders and walked to the kitchen. He found Mal there, frying some bacon.

"About time you emerged from her bedroom," he said without turning around.

He didn't sound mad, but he knew better than to trust that. Mal could be his deadliest when he was cool.

"Look. Mal…"

He trailed off when his friend turned with a smile on his face. "What are you, stupid?"

"Not following you, mate."

"Get some coffee before you fall down."

He did as ordered, watching Mal as he forked up the bacon and put it on a plate. Next, he pulled out some eggs and started cracking them into a bowl.

"See, I know you don't remember after we were evac'd out."

Hell, he could remember up until the moment he was shot. Then nothing until he woke up in the hospital.

Mal nodded. "You were completely out of it there for a while. But I remember. Once I came to, I was by your side."

He had sort of known that. Each time he had surfaced, he had seen him there by the side of his bed. "And?"

"You know the most amazing thing about being out of your mind after an injury? You don't know what you say."

It took Kade a second to figure it out. Then it hit him.

"I said something."

Mal nodded without turning around. "Over and over. You wanted to talk to Shannon."

"Shit."

"I was pretty pissed right then." He glanced back at Kade. "But, then, you were injured, and I couldn't beat the shit out of you. I wanted to, believe me. Especially since I figured out that you might have used the wedding to get her into bed."

"I wouldn't do that."

Mal stopped mixing the eggs and faced him. "Come on, Kade. I know you as well as you know me."

"And you know I'm not a slut like you."

Mal chuckled. "Yeah, you are, but it stopped about a couple of years ago. I realized then how many times you came back to New Orleans with me."

Kade couldn't help the heat that crawled into his face. Damnit, he was blushing.

"I have no idea what you're talking about." The moment he said it, he knew he sounded like an idiot.

Mal shook his head. "Son, you have got to lie better. Anyway, I realized a long time ago you had a crush on her. I ignored it for the most part because, when you have sisters like Jocelyn and Shannon, well, you're used to it. Jocelyn was always so serious, but with Shannon, well, she's got that soft heart of hers. All the guys loved to get her sympathy."

"If that's what you think attracts them and keeps them coming around, you're living in denial."

"Okay, I know it had to do with the way she's built. I'm not blind, but I can pretend. She's my sister." Mal jerked a shoulder. "Anyway, I worked through my anger. It's hard to be pissed at a guy who had his knee all fucked up, and well, knocked stupid. Stupider. I guess I should ask your intentions, but that would get me smacked around by Shannon if she found out."

76

"I'm not truly sure of my intentions."

Mal nodded in understanding. Their job didn't allow for a lot of self-reflection. Any relationship, whether sexual or not, didn't always stand up to the horrible life of the significant other of a Seal.

"I just wanted you to know I will stand clear. Shannon wouldn't have taken you to bed if she didn't want you there."

"Your sister never does anything she doesn't want to." Even Kade could hear the admiration in his own voice. He had always been drawn to strong, capable women.

"You'll get no problems from me unless you hurt her."

Kade sighed and shook his head. "Fuck, Mal, I'm a man. I'm going to hurt her."

"Not intentionally. That's different."

He nodded.

"I decided Chief and I are going out to Mama's. I really don't want to be in a house with you two. Kind of gross."

"I hope you have cheese grated for those eggs," Shannon said from the doorway. He looked in her direction, and his breath caught in his throat. The sun was now streaming in behind her. She was wearing that same little robe she was before, and he couldn't help the heat that poured into his blood at the sight of her.

"Oh, God, you two are disgusting. Can the kitchen be a non-sex part of the house?"

He glanced at his friend. "Get used to it."

Mal chuckled. "And no, I didn't put cheese into the eggs because not everyone wants it."

"My kitchen, my rules."

"But I'm not giving your boyfriend here any issues. And, remember, I am the one cooking. I won't make you any."

"You suck."

"Well, be glad I'm not going to kick your boyfriend's

ass. Because he knows I can."

She smiled at her brother then looked at Kade. "He lives in a little world of his own making, doesn't he?"

"Also, be happy I'm leaving you two alone. Chief and I are going to Mama's."

"You'll get more home-cooked meals there."

She walked over to Kade, then as if it was the most natural thing to do, slipped onto his lap. He hesitated, his chest tight at the simple gesture, and slid his arms around her waist. Chief came in next, clean-shaven, looking like he was ready to report to duty.

He gave them a disgusted look. "I still think you would be better off with me."

She laughed at that. "I'm sure you do. I need to get dressed because I have paperwork to get done."

"I thought you had off for the next few days," Kade said.

She nodded. "I forgot I have to get the schedule set up and the time sheets processed. I'll be back and there better be cheese in those eggs."

After she gave him a quick kiss, she said, "You can come with me today, but it would be really boring."

He wanted to go. He wanted to be anywhere she was. For some reason, he felt a desperate need to be in the same room as her.

The moment he thought it, he felt funny, as if something was clutching at his throat. Immediately, he backed up from that thought. They had little time together, but he needed some space. "I think the guys and I are going to go over to your mama's for lunch, or that was the plan yesterday."

Mal nodded. "Mama will be pissed if I don't bring her favorite boy."

She sighed. "Fine, abandon me for an older woman who can cook better than I could ever dream of. See where that gets you."

She slipped off his lap and went to get ready.

He rose to fill his cup when Chief said, "You know if you fuck this up, McKade, there is a good chance that after Dupree finishes with you, I'll kick your ass."

"You could try, Chief," he said cheerfully, feeling somehow lighter. He filled his cup then looked over Mal's shoulder. "Seriously, mate, you better put some cheese in those eggs."

"Shit."

· · · · ·

"You better get something to drink, Francis," Anna Louise Dupree said. He did as she told him, enjoying the homemade strawberry lemonade more than he would admit. Other than his mother, she was the only person who could get away with calling him by his first name. "And don't you worry. We'll put some meat on you this week."

He loved her as if she was his own mother, and sadly, he had a better relationship with Mal's mother. Closer. Where Jocelyn had taken after their father in looks and temperament, Shannon was her mother through and through. Her mother was average height, delightfully rounded, and so full of joy, you couldn't help but smile at her. She had taken him under her wing the moment he'd shown up with Mal several years earlier. His parents weren't bad people, they were just distant. His sister wasn't much better, not now, especially after her divorce last month. It was their nature. Their work in the field of nuclear energy was important to them, and it was the focus of most of their energy. So, when Anna Louise had hugged him like he was a long lost relative, he had been slightly overwhelmed. And, he had fallen in love with her by the end of the weekend.

"When are you going to run away with me?" he asked

as he always did.

She laughed and for a moment, he could hear Shannon. They were so much alike...except for the cooking. Her green eyes danced with merriment.

"Oh, you devil. Don't let Sam hear you, or he'll beat you up."

He snorted. "I can take your husband on."

"Maybe, but I think you might have a little trouble with my little girl, yes?"

Again his face flushed, and dammit, she laughed. It hit him then that this was the most he had spoken in weeks. Shannon and her mother were so much alike. They always drew him out of himself, got him to participate.

"I still can't believe you make this homemade, Mrs. Dupree," Deke said.

"I told you to call me Anna Louise, Deke. No one in the Dupree house stands on formality."

He smiled at her, and Mal made a sound of disgust. "It's bad enough dealing with Shannon and Kade, but do y'all have to flirt with my mother?"

"A beautiful woman like your mother should expect it," Deke said, earning him a knock to the back of the head from Mal.

"Now, you two boys go out and do something. I want to talk to Kade."

Shit. He knew that this was coming, but he hadn't been ready for it. The others agreed mainly because no one, not even Sam Dupree, said no to Anna Louise in her own house.

"Now, you going to tell me why you look like this?" She waved her hand at him.

"Bad assignment?"

She tsked. "More than that, I am sure. You brought some ghosts back with you."

He nodded, knowing there would be no denying to Anna Louise. She wouldn't allow for it.

"I'll not ask you what is bothering you. Not yet. You tell that girl of mine when you're ready."

"How does everyone know about that?"

She rolled her eyes. "What am I, stupid? Seriously, Francis, you follow her around like a puppy dog when you visit. Her brother and his friend are here at my house to stay, but not you. I know my girl has sex."

He cleared his throat. "I really don't want to talk about it."

She made a disgusted sound that he had heard a time or two from Mal. "Oh, the poor little Seal is afraid of his lover's mother." She shook her head. "Don't you talk sex with your mother?"

"Good God, no." He couldn't keep the horror out of his voice.

"Hmm, well, that might be your problem. Either way, know I do not judge. Just be careful, that's all I ask."

He looked into the eyes so similar to Shannon's and nodded. "I will do my best, Anna Louise."

She smiled then and patted his hand. "I promised that boy of mine some cornbread and fried catfish. I need help in the kitchen. You up to the challenge?"

Another thing his parents didn't know about him. He loved to cook. It had come about mainly because his parents would forget to cook. So Kade had taken over. With Anna Louise, though, he had learned so much, and she loved having him in the kitchen.

He nodded. "I'd love to."

· · · · ·

Shannon looked over the schedule for the next two weeks and sighed. She only had three more days, and the guys had to go back to Virginia. She wasn't in the mood to deal with the feelings that brought about, but in the last

three days since Kade had returned to her bed, she had
been unable to ignore them. She hadn't pushed him, hadn't
tried to. It overwhelmed her a bit too much, but it was
growing every day. She wanted to ask what he wanted
from her other than sex.

She didn't, though. She knew that at the moment, he
was doing better, but asking questions like that would be
too much. Whatever happened on the mission had really
hurt him. She had to give him time to heal, then they could
deal with what was going on between them. The
nightmares were bad, she knew without being told. And
seriously, there was another reason she hadn't pushed him.

She was being a coward.

She could wrap it up in the package of giving him time
or the idea that they were living in the moment, but it
wasn't that. She didn't push because she didn't want to
lose him.

And that was pitiful.

"You going to take the night off again?" Simon asked.
She heard the disapproval in his voice.

"Yes. They're leaving tomorrow. I don't have that
much time left with Kade."

"What's going on between you two?"

She knew what he wanted but instead she took the
chicken's way out. "I don't think I have to explain sex to
you, do I? I thought you understood all forms of it."

He frowned and shut the door behind him before
sitting down in the chair in front of her desk. "I want to
know what the hell is going to happen when he leaves."

"You and me both."

"You haven't discussed it?" he asked.

"We haven't had time to do that. Really."

Simon rolled his eyes. "Really? You're having that
much sex?"

She stared at him blankly.

"Oh, now I am jealous." Then he frowned. "Stop trying

to get me off the subject.

"You're the one who brought up sex, not me. And just so you know, Kade doesn't swing that way."

"Shannon."

She heard the reprimand in his voice. "What is it you're getting at?"

"I know he needs some help, probably has PTSD from that last mission. He's jumpy, more than usual. But, honey, you need to give yourself the right to ask for more."

"What do you mean?"

"You have always gone for what you wanted. In work, in life, with every man other than this one. You are letting him call the shots."

"Believe me, it's worth it."

"Again, stop trying to distract me with sex. You're trying to help him over what he's dealing with."

She frowned. "I don't know what he's really dealing with."

"You haven't talked about it."

She shook her head "I told you, it's only been a couple of days."

"And you think this is going to help you? Help him? I can tell by looking at him that he needs help."

"Of course he does, but do you think one of those damned Seals have spoken to me?" she asked, her voice rising. "The only thing I got out of Mal was that they lost someone, that Mal was knocked unconscious, and that's it. None of them say anything except that it was a really bad mission."

By the time she finished, she realized how loud she had gotten. The silence was almost deafening.

"Okay, so maybe they aren't ready to talk. You don't know what happened, might never. Remember, my dad was Special Forces. There are just some things they are never going to tell you. But what are you going to ask from Kade?"

Everything.

The word whispered through her mind, but she didn't say it. If she did, it wouldn't come true. She knew she was being a coward, but she had to be careful around him. Pushing him after such a traumatic situation was too much.

She opened her mouth, but Simon shook his head. "Don't say a word. I know. Just make sure that at some point, you tell him what you want. He might be hurting now, but believe me, Kade's a Seal. He can handle a few demands from you. It might be good for both of you."

When Simon finally left her alone, she realized that there was some truth to what he had been saying. She had been holding back, and she normally wouldn't. Yes, he had only been back in her life for less than a week, and their relationship had come out of a friendship. Because she had known him for years, it seemed like a long time, but it wasn't. Their sexual relationship had only been a few nights. Demanding an answer wasn't smart. It wasn't something she even wanted. Shannon knew men, she knew herself even better. She wouldn't be happy to be pushed at a time like this if she were suffering. She would give him what he needed and wait. Someday, she'd make sure he understood he had to make a choice.

She just hoped she could hold out that long.

Chapter Ten

Kade had been feeling antsy all evening. He couldn't really put his finger on it. It was as if something was crawling under his skin, urging him to some kind of action. The docs told him he would have times like this. Kade had been pretty sure the physicians had lost their minds until he came to see Shannon.

He wanted to say it was anything but the woman across the table from him. Shannon had brought home dinner from her bar, and they'd eaten by candlelight. Rain was pattering on the roof again, and there were soft blues filtering through the house. It should have been romantic. It was. Beyond romantic. She was sitting there, a smile on her face, looking like the woman of his dreams. But he couldn't shake the feeling that something really bad was about to happen.

He hated to think it was Shannon. He wanted her so much he thought he would die if he didn't touch her. At the same time, he hated himself for that. It made no sense. Any man would be happy to sit in his place and have this woman across the table smiling at him as if he were the best man on earth. He couldn't face it, didn't want to. It was their last night together, and he didn't want to ruin it with stupid thoughts.

"You done?" she asked, no reprimand in her voice.

He nodded, knowing he had been a bad dinner companion. And that irritated him more. She said nothing as she picked up the plates and took them to her sink. He watched her wash them off, then place them in the dishwasher. He was ruining the little time they had left. He was being a moody ass.

He brushed the thoughts away and rose to follow her to the sink. He stepped up behind her and placed a hand on the counter on either side of her. She stilled then leaned back against him with a purr.

"Are you back with the living?"

"Sorry."

She turned and met his gaze directly.

"Don't be. I told you, I understand. Mal does it sometimes. Dad did, every now and then. He was in Vietnam the last few years we were over there, and when I was younger, I remember he would get quiet every now and then. I realized later it was after he heard from one of his old military buddies." She rose to her tiptoes and kissed his cheek. "Don't worry so much."

The worries he did have disappeared in that kiss. It was not a sexy kiss, one that would tempt him to bed, or it wasn't meant that way. Her reassurance was more than he had expected, more than he deserved. He said nothing but reached over and turned off the water.

"Come on," he said, taking her by the hand. He led her back to her room, ready to make sure that tonight would be a night that neither of them would forget. The only light in the room was the small bedside table lamp on a low setting. Just like the woman, the room was sexy. Cool colors draped the windows, covered her bed, but it was the fabrics, the velvets and satins, that pulled him in. They weren't flowery or even overly feminine, but they were definitely sexy.

He released her and went to the dresser to retrieve the bag he'd hid by it. He'd done some shopping today, and he wanted to play. When he had laid the contents of the bag out, he turned to face her.

"I think you have too many clothes on."

She didn't look at him at first. Her gaze was latched onto the toys.

"Shannon. Look at me." She raised her gaze to his. She was worried, that was for sure. They had talked about anal sex, but had not attempted it. Tonight he wanted to show her just how much she would like it.

She undressed slowly, folding her clothes and placing them on the chair beside her dresser. If he was antsy before, he was downright ready to come undone at the moment. The soft light caressed her curves. That body...it was as if God made her for him. He undressed himself then stepped closer to her, slipping his arms around her and pulling her against him.

He bent his head and brushed his mouth over hers. His entire body reacted to the kiss. His heart sped up, his dick twitched, and his head seemed to float. Shannon would probably always do this to him. He stepped back and cupped her breast, grazing the tip of her nipple with his thumb. She was so fucking responsive.

"You better get on the bed before I lose control."

She smiled as if she didn't believe him but did as he ordered. He removed the toys from the bag and opened the tube of lube and coated the anal plug with it. "We talked about this before, and I bought the smallest one."

When he turned and faced her, he knew she would be wary. She wanted to try it, wanted to let him do what he wanted. In the last three nights, there was one thing he had learned. Shannon loved to let him take control. She was a woman who had complete control in her life, but she wanted someone else to take over in the bedroom. He approached the bed.

"Roll over, baby."

She hesitated, but did as he ordered.

"Remember your safe word if it gets too intense for you."

He slipped the toy between her ass cheeks. She

87

immediately tensed up.

"Take a deep breath and then release it slowly."

She did as he ordered, and he started easing the plug into her. He moved slowly, making sure not to hurt her. When he finally pressed it past the last ring of muscle, he let go of a breath he hadn't known he was holding.

"How does that feel?"

"Odd."

He smiled. "Turn over, but be careful."

When she was once again on her back, he went to the dresser and picked up the vibrator. "You know the rules. No coming without permission. If you do, I bought a special crop to punish you with."

She shivered, and he knew that excited her. He could just imagine slapping that generous flesh of hers with the butt plug up her ass. It was just too bad he wouldn't have time to fuck her ass. He loved it and knew she would too, but it was too soon for something like that. She wasn't ready.

He turned the vibrator on and slipped it between her legs as he bent his head and took a nipple into his mouth. She gasped when he bit down lightly on the nipple. He did the same to her other breast then rose to his knees. With his free hand, he offered her his cock.

"Take me in, baby. Suck me."

She easily complied. Shannon loved to give head, and holy shit, her mouth should be considered a lethal weapon. She slid her tongue up one side, then over the tip and down again. As she continued to tease him, she caressed his sac. God, he loved that. He usually had tight control on his sexuality, but with Shannon, he barely kept it under control. Part of it was the attraction he felt for her, the almost overwhelming need to succumb to the need that strengthened every day. He couldn't seem to understand just how she did it, how with her, he always had to hold onto his control.

He pulled back as he felt his orgasm approaching. Not yet, not when he wanted to push her to her limits.

"You can be so naughty, Shannon."

She smiled up at him, then it faded when he increased the vibrator's speed one more level, then pressed it into her pussy. The moan she gave him was one of the sweetest sounds he'd heard in a good long time.

"Remember, you aren't allowed to come. Not without my permission. You do, and I can promise you that you'll regret it."

With every word, his voice deepened and his lust was easy to hear. He was sure she heard it too.

"You are such a responsive sub. I wish we had more time to visit a club. I have a feeling you would like a little public play, wouldn't you?"

He could just imagine her there, with people watching them, having him spank her. He adjusted the vibrator, giving himself room to dip his head down between her legs. As he continued to hold the toy firm, he pulled her clit into his mouth. She moaned then, and he could tell she was close, that she was barely holding onto her control. Usually, before her, and mainly before tonight, he would push a submissive to the edge, but not over it. He always wanted to show her that she was under her control. But the punishment he had in mind had him pushing her up and over. Kade knew he was going to send her over the edge, but he wanted her to know that she was his.

He flipped a switch higher and pulled her clit between his teeth. She was fighting it. But one more graze of his teeth, and she screamed through her orgasm. She bucked so hard she pushed him off her.

Moments later, he turned off the vibrator and pulled it from between her legs. He leaned down and pushed damp curls away from her face.

"Like I said, you're a naughty girl. Do you know what I do to naughty women?"

She shook her head.

"You're about to find out. Get up on your knees, put your hands on the headboard and show me that pretty ass of yours."

He moved from the bed and placed the vibrator on the top of the dresser. Joining her back on the bed, he had to hide a smile. She was ready to take him on from the scowl on her face. She wasn't happy with him. He knew he hadn't been fair. His prerogative.

He slid the crop over her flesh, and he felt the desire surging through him. He liked the way she shivered, the way she reacted. In the past, he had subs who tried to hide their emotions from him. She never did. The connection they'd both felt from the first time they met was always there.

"Now, you might not agree with my methods. I know I'm your first Dom, but I've been a little easy on you. Really easy. If..."

He stopped himself. He couldn't talk about the time they wouldn't have. Their agreement had been to live in the moment.

He gave her little pats with the end of the crop. Shannon wiggled her ass at him, and he couldn't help but laugh.

"You really haven't learned how to behave as a sub, have you?"

She turned her head to apparently answer him, but he wasn't waiting for an answer. He pulled back the crop and smacked her. The gasp was loud, quick, and so damned erotic.

He smacked her harder and harder, making sure that no part of her ass was untouched. He skimmed his hand over her ass.

"So pretty. I used to spend hours fantasizing about your ass. If I had truly known what it looked like, I would have never been able to concentrate around you."

He gave her one little smack again, then slipped the crop between her legs, sliding it over her mons before moving away. He needed to get ahold of his control. It was slipping away. Drawing in a few breaths, he counted backwards from ten. Twice. When he finally had control, he grabbed a condom and slipped it on. He'd left her there because he'd liked the way she looked.

Now that he had control, he walked over to the bed. "Come here, honey," he said, easing her down onto the bed and onto her back. For a second, he couldn't think. She was looking up at him with those incredible eyes, her need easy to see. She was so trusting. He wanted to do nothing more than to fuck her until she couldn't remember her name. He barely held onto the savage beast that was clawing at his belly. It wanted complete power. Over her, over him, over the situation. He drew in a breath, pulling his emotions back, trying his best to conceal it from her.

He settled between her legs and then leaned closer, resting a hand on either side of her head. He could smell her arousal. She was so beautiful when she came, so lost in the pleasure. It made him want to do it again and again.

Without closing his eyes, he bent his head and kissed her, slipping his tongue between her lips. When he pulled back, she was smiling, her eyes were sultry, and her face was flush. He rose to his knees and entered her slowly. He wanted to thrust into her with no finesse. But, with the plug in her ass, he couldn't. It might be too much. She groaned in frustration.

"What? You have complaints?"

"Go faster."

He smiled at the impatience in her voice. "I am trying to be gentle."

"Be gentle later."

He should reprimand her, but he couldn't. She shouldn't be telling him what to do. At this time, though, he didn't care. He just wanted to watch her come again. He started thrusting, slowly, shallow, just enough to build her back up again. She arched up against him, and he knew what she was feeling. With the plug inside her ass, it was tighter. Each thrust took her to another level of pleasure.

Soon, she was moaning beneath him, moving in tandem with him.

He leaned down and kissed her. "Come for me, Shannon. Do it."

She was already coming by the time he finished giving her the order. Her muscles clamped down tight on him, pulling him deeper into her pussy. He kept moving, pushing himself to the release he had been needing for what seemed like forever.

She looked up at him then. Those green eyes were heavy-lidded, her lips curved, and she cupped his cheek.

"I love you, Kade."

His heart squeezed as he looked down at her and knew in that moment, she meant every word.

"Come for me," she whispered.

Her voice was so soft, he wasn't sure he heard her, but he could read her lips. He did then, thrusting into her one last time and losing himself to the pleasure.

Chapter Eleven

Darkness surrounded them. It was what they worked best in, the one thing he knew that would make it easier to extract the subject. The plan was in place, and as always, there was a backup. But Kade had a bad feeling about this one. Something in his gut was telling him that they should abort.

"Something's wrong," Mal whispered. "Really wrong."

Mal always knew when something was going down. The fact that Kade was feeling it, too, wasn't a very good sign.

Nothing moved. Not even an animal as they made their way to the rebel camp. It was so fucking hot. He just wanted to get back to Shannon. He wanted to make it out of here alive and go back to the joy he'd shared with her. Then it hit him. It was too quiet. A real base camp would at least have some kind of activity. He held his fist up, telling everyone to halt. It came a second too late. An IED went off several yards in front of them. Mal dropped to the ground and didn't move. Kade's heart was pumping hard, adrenaline coursing through him as chaos exploded around him. They all hit the dirt, and Kade crawled on the floor of the jungle to reach his friend. He was happy to find him unconscious with a steady heartbeat. Then shots were fired. He heard Forrester scream out, and he jumped to his feet. He saw a rebel holding his gun to the kid's head. Kade couldn't get a good shot off. The sound of the other gun going off echoed through the jungle.

Kade came awake screaming. Sweat rolled down his back, and in the coolness of the room, he shivered. His heart was smacking against his ribs.

"Kade? Are you okay?" Shannon asked, her soft voice filled with sleep and worry.

Still feeling the raw from the dream, he said nothing, just rose from the bed and went into the bathroom.

By the time he returned, she had turned on her bedside light and pulled on her robe.

"Do you want to talk about it?"

"Nothing to talk about."

She frowned. "You have nightmares every night. Talking sometimes helps."

"Well, it won't help me. Just forget it."

He settled back in the bed. He didn't want to look at her, couldn't.

"Have you talked to anyone about it?"

"Let it go, Shannon. I'm not in the mood."

He closed his eyes but the light remained on. He sighed and opened his eyes and found her watching him. She was still rumpled from sleep, her hair a tangle of curls down her back. With a smile, he set his hand on her thigh. "I do know what will help me sleep."

Her eyes softened, but she shook her head. "I really do think you need to talk about it. I know having nightmares after a mission is routine, but it's been months. I know when I talk about mine, they don't seem so scary."

He removed his hand from her leg and fought back the panic that rose to his throat. "I'm not scared. Just a messed up dream."

"If you don't face your problem how are you going to fix—"

"Is this about you fixing me?"

Irritated and needing space, he rose from the bed. He pulled on his pants.

94

"What do you mean by that?"

"I should have known you weren't being truthful. Women are always trying to fix men. You think that you know what's best for us. I don't need any help working through my issues. I'm fine."

The silence in the room had him panicking. When he turned to face her, he was sure he would find her crying, but instead, she was staring at him. Expressionless.

"I was just offering a suggestion, but apparently, I hit a nerve."

He didn't like the way she looked now. As if she had shut down. She was normally so full of life. The contrast was stunning. The fact that it was his fault pissed him off even more. He knew it was wrong. He knew he was digging his grave. Still, he went on.

"No, what you're trying to do is tell me how to live."

She opened her mouth, then snapped it shut. She shut down even more. If she was expressionless before, she was downright icy cold.

"Fine."

She scooted out of bed and moved away from him. His panic increased, and with it, his anger.

"That's what's wrong with women. Always trying to fix us."

"I believe you already mentioned that. I have never tried to fix you, or whatever you're talking about." Her voice was low when she spoke, and he knew her temper was getting the better of her. "In fact, I have walked on eggshells around you since you showed up. It has been only a few days, and I have never asked what was coming up next. Never."

"You were too busy trying to make sure you took care of me."

She stared at him as if he had grown a second head. "You're pissed at me because I cared for you?"

When she said it that way, it made him sound like an

ass. He pushed that thought aside. He might only have his pride right now, well not much of it, but some.

"That's not the real problem, though, is it, you stupid Seal? You want to control everything. All the time. Is that why you can't sleep through the night anymore? You went on a mission and things got out of control? So you found out you have no power in a lot of situations. Worse, you can't control me. "

"That has nothing to do with it."

"Because I didn't act like some kind of clinging vine, you had to come up with another reason that I was ruining your life. Fine. Run. Be the coward."

"What did you call me?" he asked. His temper was growing as the panic dissolved.

"You heard me. I'm willing to love you, give you all my love, but you are being such a thickheaded Seal, you can't accept that. Fine. Go. Get out of my house."

"Where the hell am I supposed to go?"

"I have no idea, just get out of my room."

He hesitated, trying to figure out if she was serious. From the fire sparking in her green eyes, he was pretty damned sure she wanted him to leave. He was just glad she didn't believe in owning a handgun. He would worry about what appendage she would shoot off.

"Fine."

Without another word, he walked to the door. Something had his stomach churning, and it wasn't the nightmare. He slammed the door behind him and walked to the guest room. He knew he was probably wrong. What did his father always say? Men are always wrong if there was a woman involved.

Fuck. He had lashed out at her because of his own issues and hurt her. He walked out into the hall again and stopped at her door. He heard her then, the loud sobs piercing his heart. He pressed his hand against the door, wanting nothing more than to go in and hold her. But it would be false. He wasn't truly cut out for this. He would hurt her again. And in the end, she would hate him more than she did now.

Feeling impotent, he turned and walked away. Each step he took hurt him more than his damaged knee. Knowing he loved her with every step was killing him, but a woman like Shannon deserved a whole man.

He would never be able to offer her that again.

. . . . .

Shannon went through the motions of saying her goodbyes. She didn't like big emotional scenes, not when no good could come out of them. Kade was going to believe what he wanted, and in the time they'd had, they couldn't work through their problems. And he didn't want to. While she and Kade barely spoke, she did say goodbye.

"You want to tell me what happened there?" Mal asked when they were alone.

"He's a pig-headed fool."

He studied her for a second. "I can beat him up."

"That's sweet." She gave him a kiss. "Your buddy there beats himself up enough. Maybe one day he'll come to his senses. Though, he is a man. So there is a good a chance that he will never come to his senses. You *are* the lesser sex."

He sighed. "Okay, but call me if you change your mind. I can make his life hell."

She nodded. "Stay safe. Please."

He nodded and gave her another kiss on the cheek, and then strode toward the car. Kade refused to look at her. He had mumbled his goodbyes, but she hadn't been truly open to conversation with him, either. She watched as her brother pulled away from the curb and said a little prayer for the three men for their journey, and lord, whatever mission they next went on. She walked back into her house, shutting the door and walking to the kitchen. Shannon was cried out. She didn't think she had another tear left in her.

Her phone rang, and when she saw the eight-oh-eight area code, she frowned. It was the middle of the night for her sister.

"What are you doing up?"

"No hello, Jocelyn? I miss you."

Her chest clutched and near tears formed in her eyes. "I do love you, you know that, you idiot."

Jocelyn sighed. "Malachai called. You need to talk?"

She sniffed. "Yeah, I do."

She heard someone talking in the background and knew it was Kai.

"Kai said he could beat him up for you."

Shannon chuckled through her tears. "Malachai already offered, and since they have to spend two days in the car together, he'll have more of a chance."

"So tell me about it."

She wanted to. She wanted nothing more than to sit down and talk to the one person she was closest to in the world. "I will, but I think I want to do it in person. You up for a guest for a couple of weeks?"

"Always. My father-in-law has been testing out his two-stepping on the women at the community center, but he says you are the only one who does it right."

"I would really like that. I would like that a lot."

"You make your plans then let me know."

"Sure. I have to arrange everything at the bar, but I'll let you know."

"Love you, Shan."

"I love you, Jocey."

When she hung up, she took a deep breath, and before she could think differently, she pulled out the phone and called Simon. She needed to get away, and she needed her sister.

. . . . .

Kade cursed the moment he tried to do a roundhouse kick to the punching bag. His knee almost crumbled under his weight.

"Looking good there, Kade," Mal said.

He glanced at his friend who was using the bag next to him. Since they had returned the week before, he hadn't tried to ask Kade anything. Hadn't accused him or tried to kick his ass. It was making him nervous. His friend was mad. He knew that. But he was holding back.

"I could kick your ass any day of the week."

Mal scoffed. "You? You're afraid of a little woman."

The area of the gym where they stood went silent. Kade glanced around at the other Seals. They were watching them as if a show was about to begin.

He turned back to Mal. "What did you say?"

Mal rolled his shoulders. "You're afraid of Shannon."

There were a few whispers as he felt his temper rising. "Did she tell you that?"

"No, but she did call you a pig-headed idiot, or something like that. She didn't have to tell me. I could see you running away from her."

"Go fuck yourself."

"Gladly. If you can stop being a pain in the ass to everyone here."

Kade glanced around at the crowd that had gathered and realized that some of the guys were shaking their heads. He could feel anger whipping through him, crawling into his head and taking control of his better judgment.

"You itching for a fight?" he asked. He was ready for it, needed it, craved it. He took a step toward him.

"McKade! Dupree!"

They both turned around to find the leader of the group staring at them. *Fuck.*

"My office, now."

Without a word between them, they pulled off their gloves and followed the Lieutenant Commander to his office.

"You two want to tell me what the fuck is going on?"

Neither of them said a word.

"I can't have my men fighting like a bunch of idiots. We're still trying to piece the group back together, and you two have to act like ten-year-olds on the playground. I really don't want to do the fucking paperwork involved if I have to discipline. Can you assure me that you will behave like Seals from now on? I would hate to transfer one of you out of here."

Kade knew without a doubt it would be him. He was trying to recover, and Mal was in working order.

They both nodded.

"Dupree, you can go."

His friend tossed him a sympathetic look. When the door shut, Markinson said, "Sit."

Shit, this was going to take a while. They were never offered a seat unless it was going to be a long chat. Still, he did as ordered, fighting the pain that shot through his leg.

"McKade, I know that we don't do the feeling thing. We're men, and worse, we're Seals. But you have got to get the bug that crawled up your ass out of there. From the moment you came back from leave, you have been a pain in the ass. For me, for everyone around you. I thought you would at least be relaxed after a week in New Orleans. You were worse. We'll be on active status again, and I need to know that I can count on you. The men need to know."

"I'll be ready."

100

He sighed. "I don't want to know what you're feeling, seriously. But, you were closed off for so long, and now you're bitching at everyone. Yes, I used the word bitching. You got in a fight with Smith because he didn't load his weapon right. It's like you've lost your center."

The moment Markinson said it, the image of Shannon came to his mind. She always centered him. Even before they were involved, he could chat with her as a friend and feel his life get back on track. She was the one thing that he needed to make it work, and he had pushed her away. No wonder he'd been acting like a raving lunatic. Without Shannon, he had no compass.

"Are you listening to me?"

He blinked at his commander.

"Uh, yes, sir."

"I understand what it's like to lose someone. I was in Fallujah as you know. So...it was bad. But, you have to work through it. Go see a doctor, get some meds."

Fuck. What a great time to figure out that pushing Shannon away was what had left him screwed up. The mission had been painful, losing his friend bad. It was the worst. Or he thought. Now that he didn't have Shannon, he didn't think straight. He couldn't even work through his emotions.

"Permission to be excused, sir."

Markinson stopped in midsentence and looked up at him.

"I was talking here, McKade."

"I understand. I just figured out what I needed to fix something."

He continued to study Kade. "Okay, but just know I need you one hundred percent by the end of four weeks."

Kade nodded. "Oh, and I need to take off a week."

"What? Another one?" he asked, almost shouting.

"I just figured out what I needed."

"And it takes you a week to fix it?"

"No. It will take me a week to convince her to take me back."

Understanding filled the commander's eyes. "You got it. Good luck."

With more purpose than he'd felt in months, he walked out of the office and walked down the hall. Mal stepped out of the locker room.

"Look, Kade, I'm sorry. I shouldn't have picked that fight with you. Did Markinson bust your ass?"

"No." He started toward the door. "Can you take me to the airport?"

"Wait. What?"

Kade hurried down the stairs and ignored the chill in the air and pain in his knee. Now that he knew what he wanted to do, where he wanted to be, he needed to get to Shannon now.

"I'm flying to New Orleans."

"Why?"

"To get on my knees and beg."

"Shannon isn't there."

He stopped in his tracks and looked up at Mal. "Where is she?"

"Hawaii. She left a couple days ago to spend some time with Jocelyn."

He huffed out a breath. "Okay, I need to move some money around, and then I'm flying to Hawaii."

Mal shook his head. "Do you know what you're doing?"

"Yeah, dammit." He started walking again. "I'm going to get my woman."

Chapter Twelve

Shannon sighed as she picked at her food. Chris had been making all her favorite foods, including the Huli Huli chicken and rice she wasn't eating at the moment. From the moment Kade had left her that morning, she'd hadn't felt like eating. She still didn't have an appetite, which was worrisome.

"You need to eat."

She looked up at her brother, who was studying her as if she were going to fall apart. Okay, so she cried the first three days she was there, but she was done. Sort of. And sure, she hadn't wanted to talk to any men. Not even Evan, whom she adored.

"I'm just not that hungry."

He shook his head. "I told Cynthia that you weren't eating enough."

"And what did she say?"

"She said I was used to being with a woman who ate enough for five people."

Jocelyn laughed. "She looks ready to explode."

"Don't say that around her. I had to help her get her tennis shoes on yesterday. She cried for an hour."

She smiled at her brother. "Aw, and you couldn't take it, you old softie."

He grimaced then he frowned as his attention was drawn to something behind her. "What the fuck is he doing here?"

Her brother didn't cuss that much, at least not in front

of her. She turned to follow his line of vision and saw Kade.

Her breath tangled in her throat, and her heart started beating so fast she was amazed she didn't pass out.

He looked wonderful—damn him. He was dressed in his service dress. He freaking looked like freaking Richard Gere. The restaurant had grown quiet. She was sure you didn't see a Navy Seal in full dress whites march into a local business on a regular basis in Honolulu.

He was looking around, and just for a second, she thought about slipping down in the booth and hiding. She wasn't ready to deal with the churning emotions he brought about in her. A moment later, though, he caught sight of her and started in her direction. Lord, he was a sight to see. There was nothing like a Seal on a mission, and apparently, she was his mission.

He strode toward her, every step sending panic racing through her.

"What the hell is he doing here?" she asked more to herself than anyone else.

"I don't give a damn," Chris muttered as he stood. "I'm going to kill him."

She stood up and faced her brother. She loved him with all her heart, but she knew Kade and knew what he could do.

"I can take care of this."

His frown turned darker. "I don't want you to."

"I can handle it. Besides, I do not want to help Cynthia raise that baby because you're in a wheelchair for the rest of your life."

"You don't think I could handle him?" Pure astonishment filled his tone.

"Sure you can. Working behind a stove and running a restaurant gets you in shape to take on a killing machine like a Seal."

He made a face. "Okay, you have a point."

She patted his cheek then turned to face Kade.

He stopped within a few feet of her and stared. The moment got awkward as he continued to gaze at her as if she were his salvation. He looked better, rested, and for a moment, she hated him for that. She hadn't had a good night's sleep in three weeks, and here he was looking like a million bucks.

She could feel everyone still looking at them. Something had to give, so she did what every Dupree knew how to do. She joked.

"Kind of dressed up for the occasion, Kade?'

He didn't say anything, but his lips twitched.

She crossed her arms beneath her breasts. "You flew all the way over here to stare at me?"

He shook his head, but his gaze didn't leave hers. "I came for you."

Her heart did that little happy dance, but she pushed it away. She didn't want this, didn't want to deal with the hurt again. She thought she could, thought she could be patient while he worked himself out, but she realized that she might not be cut out to have a Seal as a lover.

"No."

He frowned.

"No?"

Poor pitiful Seal.

"Yeah, I said no. Just because you put on a uniform and march into my brother's restaurant doesn't mean I'm going to forget everything."

He glanced around at their audience. "Shouldn't we talk about this in private?"

"You picked the setting."

"You tell him, sistah," someone yelled out.

He grimaced. "I thought we would go for a walk."

Oh, he looked miserable. Just so miserable. He might love her, but flying across the Pacific didn't really prove it. She wanted more, she wanted it all. And the only way she

105

could get it was if she knew that he was in it for the long haul, like she was.

"Thinking's overrated."

A few more of the customers started catcalling, and his face started to turn pink. Oh, my. He was embarrassed. And there was a tiny, evil part of her that was happy he was.

"I wanted to talk to you about our future."

"We don't have one."

Up until that moment, he had been what she would call docile—for a Seal. Now his eyes turned hard, his jaw flexed. She had to fight the urge to step back away from him. She had never been scared of him, but at the moment, she could easily see his anger.

"Don't say that."

Even though she could tell he was angry, she could hear a thread of desperation in his voice. It pricked at the already melting ice that encased her heart.

"You're the one who ran away."

He sighed. "I was stupid."

She wanted to punish him, but since he admitted he was stupid, she would at least be cordial. "From the uniform, I assume you're going to stay in the military?"

He nodded.

"So you flew over, and that must have been expensive by the way, dressed up in your little white uniform, to tell me you're staying in the military."

"I came for you."

The declaration had a few of the women sighing, and if she were honest with herself, Shannon's heart did a little flip flop.

"Me? Oh, the person who was trying to fix you?"

His jaw flexed again. "You were right, I was scared. Mainly because my mortality had been in question."

"We're all mortal."

"He *is* a Seal, Shannon," her brother said from behind

her.

She glanced over her shoulder with narrowed eyes. "Stay out of this, or I'll tell Cynthia you told me about helping her with her shoes."

He held up his hands in self-defense.

When she turned back to Kade, she was still frowning. She had to stay mad. It was her only safety from falling for the idiot again.

"As I was saying, that last mission was bad. Really bad. I knew it was, and so did Mal, but we didn't act fast enough. I...well, I questioned if I was fit to serve."

Oh, God, he was killing her. He had been like Mal. The only reason he had gotten into the military was to be a Seal. It had been the thing that had driven them, the one thing they identified with the most.

"Just because you had one bad mission doesn't mean that you should quit. You're a good Seal."

He nodded. "Since taking you to bed, I care more about being a good man."

She couldn't take this. Her heart was melting, her better judgment flying out the window with the trade winds. If she gave into him, what would she do?

"You *are* a good man." Her voice was raw with emotion. She might not be able to take him back, but there was one thing she knew. He was good at his core. Always had been.

He nodded, then bent down on one knee. Several of the women gasped, and there was a patter of applause.

"I love you, Shannon. Will you marry me?"

Panic came first. It took her by the throat and would not let go. She couldn't speak, couldn't swallow the lump in her throat. Then on the heels of it came anger. He thought he could propose and everything would be okay.

"No."

"What did you say?"

"You can't just come in here with a ring..." When she

noticed him grimace, she realized he wasn't offering her a ring. "You didn't even bring a ring, you idiot." She slapped him on the shoulder and went to move past him, but Kade grabbed her by the wrist.

"I thought you'd want to pick one out."

The moment he touched her, her pulse jumped. Fear had her twisting her arm free. She wasn't afraid of him, but of what she would do. She couldn't say yes, deal with the idiot's moods. Months of waiting for him to come home, then have to joke him out of his stupid bad mood and God, hear him laugh as he hugged her.

Tears stung her eyes. She did not want that. No way.

"No. Stay away."

He rose to his feet and started after her. She was heading for the door with no idea of where she was going. She left her purse behind, she didn't have a car, but she just needed to get away.

Her hand was inches from the door when he scooped her up off the floor, then positioned her on his shoulder like a freaking sack of potatoes.

"You know, woman, I had to chase you across the Pacific. I came to apologize, to tell you I love you, to tell you I want to spend my life with you, and what do you do? You say no and run away."

"Put. Me. Down."

He apparently heard the threat in her voice and decided to heed the tone. He slowly put her down. She stepped back from him, but put up her hand when he inched closer.

"I promise not to leave. Just...stay there."

If he was close, she would feel his warmth, take in his scent, and she couldn't handle that. Her head was already spinning.

"Why are you running?"

The question had her stomach churning. She *was* running. She wasn't going to admit it to him.

"I just wanted to get away. I needed some space. I

don't like public declarations."

He cocked his head, then that slow smile that always melted her bones curved his lips. "You're afraid."

"Go to hell."

She turned to march away, but he caught her and pulled her back against him.

"I'm sorry, baby. So sorry. You didn't take any cheap shots at me, and I shouldn't have been so happy about you being scared."

"I'm not scared." But even as she said it, she knew she was lying.

"Yeah, you are. It's okay. This thing we have is scary."

He turned her gently and cupped her face, wiping away the tears from her cheeks.

"I want to marry you, I want to have babies with you, but know I have to finish my obligation. I have four more years, then I'm out."

"You'll stay in more."

He shook his head. "I love it, really do. But…I love you more. I need you more than I need this. It's a lot to ask. I'll be in Virginia, then out in the field. You'll be in New Orleans. But, we can make this work. I know we can."

She sighed, her heart just falling down at his feet then. It wasn't so much of what he said, but the way he said it, and the soft look in his eyes.

"I have to ask again, because, Shannon, without you, being a Seal means nothing to me. I love you. Please, marry me."

Her vision blurred as another batch of fresh tears filled her eyes. "Oh, Kade, I love you, too. Yes. Yes! I'll marry you."

He pulled her into his arms and kissed her as the sound of customer's applause filled the air.

Epilogue

"What do you have planned?" Shannon asked as Kade took her hand and led her out of the elevator.

"You're the worst about secrets. I thought you were bad at Christmas." She could hear the smile in his voice, but she couldn't see him. He'd blindfolded her downstairs and refused to tell her where they were going. She knew they were still in the hotel where they had their wedding reception, but she wasn't sure where they were going.

"For all I know, you're leading me down the hallway to kill me."

"No, I just have a surprise, and I didn't want you to know about it."

She frowned at that as he stopped her. She opened her mouth to tell him just what she thought, but she heard a woman's delighted squeal in the distance.

"What the hell?" Kade said.

"Was it someone we knew?"

"It looked like Deke with some blonde. Doesn't matter."

She heard him unlock a door, then he guided her inside. The scent of plumeria hit her first along with the sensual scents that she knew to be candles. He stepped behind her, untied her blindfold, and removed it from her eyes.

Candles covered almost every available surface. On the bedside table, the dresser. It was the only light in the room. The bed was covered with plumeria petals. Tears filled her eyes. She recognized the room.

"This was my room for the night of Chris and Cynthia's wedding."

He slid his arms around her waist and pulled her back against him. He brushed his lips against her jaw. "Yep. I had to pull a few strings to make sure we got it. And Jocelyn helped me. She snuck up here a few minutes ago and got it ready."

She smiled, thinking of her sister and the surprise she had for her husband tonight. She turned in Kade's arms and cupped his face. He had been gorgeous at the ceremony, dressed in the same uniform he'd proposed to her in. But now he was dressed in a Hawaiian shirt and a pair of chinos, and he was just as delicious.

"I am the luckiest woman in the world."

His smile faded as he touched his forehead to hers. "No, love. You can't be with a bloke like me. I put you through some hard times. I'm sorry that I'm going to probably put you through some more. Being a military wife isn't easy."

"No, it's not. But it's the only kind of wife I want to be."

He kissed her then, sweet, hot, and by the time he was finished, they were both breathing heavily. Stepping away, he took her hand. "Come, let me love you."

She followed him to the bed, laying down first. He stood looking at her for a moment.

"You have no idea how amazing you look."

"Yeah?"

"Decadence and innocence all rolled up into one delicious woman."

She didn't think she would ever get used to the way he spoke to her. He might be a quiet one, but when those words flowed over her, they took hold of her heart and would not let go.

"Well, come on, Seal, I think we need to explore that

decadent side."

The naughty smile he gave her told Shannon he had more than a little decadence planned for the night.

He joined her on the bed then pulled her into his arms. He rolled them across the mattress so that she was beneath his powerful body.

"Well, Mrs. McKade—"

"I like the sound of that," she said.

"I do too." He brushed his mouth over hers before he slid down her body. "And I am ready to show you just how much I love the fact that you're *my* Mrs. McKade."

"Oh, yeah?"

He inched the hem of her wedding dress up over her thighs, his eyes widening when he saw that she hadn't worn any panties.

She laughed. "Oh, my, I think I shocked you."

He shook his head, his gaze directly on her pussy. He skimmed his fingers over her mons, then dipped two into her sex. She shivered.

"That was very naughty, Shannon."

She heard the change of tone, knew that he was already getting into full Dom mode.

He bent his head and licked her slit then said, "Now, remember, baby. No coming until I say you can."

Then, he set about driving her insane as she lay on a bed of petals in the room where they fell in love.

The End

Coming in digital May 2012 the next military romance from Melissa Schroeder...

Possession: A Little Harmless Military Romance

Deke Berg has been in love with Sam for ten years. From the moment they met, they could never keep their hands off each other. Their marriage was volatile and short-lived, and they were both much too young. Now, though, Deke knows what he wants in life, and Sam is at the center of his plans. Unfortunately, Sam is wary of marriage--especially to a man who broke her heart.

Sam has always loved Deke. Being a former military brat, she thought she'd been prepared for life as a military spouse. But the long separations were hard, especially dealing with the stranger who returned home. When he refused to get help, she left and always regretted it. She doesn't know if she can handle that pain again, but after spending a night together in Hawaii it's impossible for her to ignore him.

Old prejudices and painful memories aren't easy to overcome, but there is one thing Deke understands: Sam is the woman for him and he will do *anything* to prove his love and win her back.

Warning, this book includes: Another hard-headed military man, a few embarrassing moments, nosey brothers, and two people too stupid to realize they are perfect together. It's Harmless and military, so for your own safety make sure you have ice water nearby. The author assumes no responsibility for overheating of the reader.

Enjoy the following unedited excerpt from
Possession: A Little Harmless Military Romance:

He skimmed his fingers up her arms. "We said we wouldn't do this again."

She drew in a deep breath then released it with a sigh of pleasure as he skimmed his fingers over her pulse. "We always say we won't do it again."

He looked up at her, those grey eyes dark with need for her. His lips curved slowly. Her heart did the slow roll it did right before it fell at his feet.

"I have a really nice room with a great view."

She laughed. "Really?"

"Yeah, why don't I show you?" He stepped back and held out his hand. She looked down at it, knew that this was her decision. This time, it was all up to her.

She looked at him and smiled. It was insane and it was really stupid, but just like always, she couldn't resist him. All of the barriers she had built crumbled when she saw the curve of his lips. There was something wrong with her—with both of them—but she didn't matter.

Without a word, she threw away all her worries and took his hand. He raised it to his mouth. Keeping his gaze on hers he touched his lips to her fingers.

"Come with me."

About Melissa Schroeder

Born to an Air Force family at an Army hospital Melissa has always been a little bit screwy. She was further warped by her years of watching Monty Python and her strange family. Her love of romance novels developed after accidentally picking up a Linda Howard book. After becoming hooked, she read close to 300 novels in one year, deciding that romance was her true calling instead of the literary short stories and suspenses she had been writing. Since her first release in 2004, Melissa has had over 30 short stories, novellas and novels released with multiple publishers in a variety of genres and time periods. Those releases include the Harmless series, a best-selling erotic romance series set in Hawaii. A Little Harmless Sex, book 1, was one of the top 100 bestselling Nook Books of 2010.

Since she was a military brat, she vowed never to marry military. Alas, fate always has her way with mortals. Her husband is an Air Force major, and together they have their own military brats, two girls, and two adopted dog daughters, and they live wherever the military sticks them. Which she is sure, will always involve heat and bugs only seen on the Animal Discovery Channel. In her spare time, she reads, complains about bugs, travels, cooks, reads some more, watches her DVD collections of Arrested Development and Seinfeld, and tries to convince her family that she truly is a delicate genius. She has yet to achieve her last goal.

You can connect with Mel all over the web:

www.melissaschroeder.net
www.twitter.com/melschroeder
www.facebook.com/melissaschroederfanpage
www.facebook.com/groups/harmlesslovers

Or email her at: Contact@MelissaSchroeder.net

Other Books by Melissa Schroeder

Harmless

A Little Harmless Sex
A Little Harmless Pleasure
A Little Harmless Obsession
A Little Harmless Lie
A Little Harmless Addiction
A Little Harmless Submission
A Little Harmless Fascination

A Little Harmless Military Romance

Infatuation

The Harmless Shorts

A Little Harmless Fling—Free on Website
A Little Harmless Kalikimaka—Free on Website
A Little Harmless Surprise-Free on ARE/Smashwords
A Little Harmless Gift-Free on ARE/Smashwords

Once Upon An Accident

The Accidental Countess
Lessons in Seduction
The Spy Who Loved Me

Leather and Lace

The Seduction of Widow McEwan
Leather and Lace—Print anthology

Texas Temptations

Conquering India
Delilah's Downfall

Hawaiian Holidays

Mele Kalikimaka, Baby
Sex on the Beach
Getting Lei'd

Bounty Hunters, Inc

For Love or Honor
Sinner's Delight

The Sweet Shoppe

Tempting Prudence—free on website
Turning Paige

Connected Books

Seducing the Saint
Hunting Mila
Saints and Sinners—print of both books
The Hired Hand
Hands on Training
Cancer Anthology

Water—print

Stand Alone Books

Grace Under Pressure
The Last Detail
Her Mother's Killer
A Calculated Seduction
Telepathic Cravings

Coming Soon

Possession: A Little Harmless Military Romance
A Little Harmless Fantasy
Surrender: A Little Harmless Military Romance
By Blood: Desire
The Cursed Clan: Angus
A Little Harmless Ride
Craving: A Little Harmless Military Romance
Relentless: A Little Harmless Military Romance
A Little Harmless Secret
Falling in Love Again
A Lethal Woman
Going for Eight

Writing as Kiera West exclusively for Siren
Publishing

The Great Wolves of Passion, Alaska

Seducing Their Mate
The Alpha's Fall
Convincing Ethan
Shane's Need
Rand's Craving

Coming soon

Jason's Salvation
Max's Need
Claiming Their Mate

Now Available in digital from Melissa Schroeder

Wanting her isn't smart, seducing her is inevitable, but falling in love with her could be downright deadly for both of them.

A Little Harmless Fascination
Harmless Book 7

Security expert Conner Dillon isn't a man who often takes a vacation. So when he is ordered to take a month off and his sister insists on a trip to Hawaii, he isn't very happy. But, after seeing his landlady Jillian Sawyer again, he might just find something—or someone—to occupy his time.

For years, Jillian has always had a crush on Conner. Now an erotic romance author with a thing for Doms, she finds herself beyond intrigued by the man. He is good to the core, but there is something else darker in him that calls to her.

After one night in bed, they both find themselves addicted. In Jillian, Conner has found the perfect sub…and in him she finds someone she can trust. Falling in love isn't what they expected, but walking away is impossible—especially when they realize someone wants Jillian dead.

WARNING this book contains the following: An uptight security expert who prefers schedules, a romance writer who does not, tattoos, a trip to the Aloha Swap Meet, and of course this would not be a Harmless book without a trip to Rough 'n Ready. Ice is recommended as any Harmless Addict will tell you, but the author takes no responsibility if a reader should become overheated. Read at your own risk.

Enjoy the following unedited excerpt from *A Little Harmless Fascination:*

She had been right. He had been flirting with her. That thought made most of her brain melt on the spot. When she finally gathered enough of her wits to answer, he'd moved closer, resting his hand on her car behind her. She could smell him, that musky scent of his aftershave and…Conner. It took all her control not to lean in and sniff him.

"Yeah. But then, I know just how fast to go."

His expression hardened and even in the dim light, she could see the flush on his cheeks. Knowing she was getting to him had her libido revving out of control.

"Do you know what you're messing with?"

She slipped closer. "I think that's who not what."

His mouth curved. He slid his arm around her waist pulled her close and kissed her.

At first the kiss was gentle, then he deepened it, plunging his tongue between her lips. Everything in her yearned, wanted, needed. This man had been hitting all the points for days and now, she craved him.

He moved and pressed his body against her. She would have to be dead not to feel his erection.

By the time he pulled back, her head was spinning and her heart was beating so hard, she thought she might pass out. Lord, the man was deadly with his mouth.

"Answer me one question."

She couldn't seem to open her eyes.

"Jillian, open your eyes." When she didn't respond, he snapped out, "Now."

She did as he ordered before she even thought about it.

"Were you at Rough 'n Ready for fun or was it really research for a book?"

She smiled knowing it would irritate him. She wanted to push him just to see his reaction and it would do to her. "A little of both."

He didn't like that answer. She could tell by the way his eyes narrowed as he studied her. "I don't think you know what you're getting yourself into."

"Why don't you tell me about it, Conner."

She heard the challenge in her voice, knew that she was definitely hitting some hot buttons for him.

He crowded her against her car again. The heat of him surrounded her and she wanted another kiss. Another taste of the paradise she knew he would be able to offer her. Conner leaned down.

When his mouth was within a centimeter of hers, he said, "When you want to do more than play games, you let me know, Jillian."

Please visit MelissaSchroeder.net for more info!

Enjoy the first chapter of Melissa Schroeder's upcoming historical paranormal romance coming to digital and print this July:

A man with a secret.

Nicodemus Blackburn has seen the best and worst of mankind. Five hundred years of dealing with them teaches the vampire to be very wary of the creatures. Unfortunately, alarming events leave him no choice but to enter the world of the ton to hunt a rogue vampire—one who is making his own army of blood thirsty vampires. Searching for the villain is not the worst of his troubles. That can be laid at the feet of bluestocking Lady Cordelia Collingsworth.

A woman on a mission.

Cordelia has always been an outcast, even in her own family. She has forged her way in the world with her ability to write, and Nico Blackburn is the focus of her next article. Before she can obtain any information about the mysterious man, she is pulled headlong into a scandal that leaves her with no choice but to marry Nico—a man with dangerous secrets.

A passion that consumes them both.

Thrust into a world she knows nothing of, Cordelia finds herself falling in love with a man who claims to be a vampire. As their passion grows, so does the danger around them and Nico will have to call on all of his powers to protect the one thing he has realized he cannot live without: his opinionated, infuriating, and thoroughly delectable wife.

By Blood: Desire

Prologue

Late in Queen Victoria's Reign
"He was Made?" Malik asked.

Nicodemus Blackburn did not look at his friend, but nodded and continued to clean the blood from beneath his fingernails. The only sound in the dank room was the splashing of water.

"How old?"

"I would say less than two months. Definitely not completely transitioned."

Silence. When Malik didn't respond, Nico glanced at him. His friend's face passive, his eyes cold. They had learned long ago Malik would be the whipping boy for every damned Made vampire.

"He was completely out of control. The woman..." Nico closed his eyes and swallowed back the fresh wave of nausea that threatened to bubble up. In five hundred years, he had never seen anything so brutal, so bestial. He had killed Mades before, but never happened upon one of their kills. He opened his eyes to find his friend with a knowing look on his face. "She did not die easily."

If possible, Malik's expression grew colder. "Meaning he raped her to death."

There was nothing to be said, for nothing would stop what was going to happen, what was already happening. Nico grabbed a linen cloth and started to dry his hands.

"We need to find out what the bloody hell is happening. This one had no connection to family. There has to be a reason for the Made vampires to be popping up all over the countryside"

Malik nodded. "I've heard more rumbling amongst the Borns. Not to mention the Carrier woman they found dead in London two nights ago. There might be trouble for my kind again."

Nico shrugged and retrieved another shirt. "I don't think you need to worry."

"Don't lie."

"You are always exempt from these witch hunts. You trace your roots back further than mine. Anyone who has made it through transition has no problem. They never lose control."

A cynical smile curved Malik's lips. "True. And so I shouldn't have to worry at all. But the youngest generation doesn't remember the Inquisition...they don't remember how many of us fought on your side. They will be out for blood."

Nico faced him. Irritation and worry gripped his stomach in a cold, hard fist. What Malik said was true. Before the Inquisition, the Borns regularly hunted for Mades, killing them before they gained control of their new powers. He could not defend what had happened in the past, only work to fix the present.

But, that would come later. Nico could still smell the corpse's blood on his body. If he closed his eyes he could remember everything. The mutilation of the Carrier woman, the sickening feel of shoving a piece of wood into the vampire's flesh. The word Suprema still echoed in his ears.

It was worse than it had been almost four hundred years ago. God, he did not want to do that ever again. But he would...he knew that down to his core. There was no way to avoid it. If he allowed someone else to lead the hunt, it would become a massacre of every Made vampire in England.

He opened his eyes and looked at his best friend. They had seen the worst mankind could throw at them and the worst. Nico feared they were about to see things neither of them were prepared for.

"The trail leads to London," Malik said.

"Yes. My father agrees."

"Your father is the only family leader with any intelligence."

True, for he was the oldest of the four family patriarchs that comprised the vampire clans of England and Scotland.

"In father's mind, he is the only one who matters. But, in this case he is correct. London would be easier...the maker could resort to the lower classes and it would not attract any attention."

"Do you have any idea who it might be?"

Nico shook his head. "Not a clue. All I know is the sightings in the country have dwindled and those we have found all lead to London."

"I hate London."

Nico smiled at his friend's irritation. Both of them hated London, the ton and all of their idiocy. But his father had asked him to go, and Nico could not refuse. "We go to London."

Malik studied him for a moment, and then nodded. "We go to London."

Chapter One

He was avoiding her again.

Lady Cordelia Collingsworth searched through the milling crowd in the Smyth's ballroom as irritation shot through her blood. This was the third night in a row he had lost her. The mysterious man was making it impossible to discover anything about him...or his shady businesses.

"Lady Cordelia."

She grimaced before she could stop herself. Viscount Hurst. He had been dogging her steps at every event for the last fortnight. He always appeared at her side, a genial smile on his face, and pretty compliments. Drat the man. She smoothed her expression and turned to face the viscount.

Cordelia understood why he had been labeled "The Catch" by the ladies of the ton early this season. Just thirty years old, he sported a strong physique. Blonde hair and deep brown eyes had all the women sighing, or so she had been told. He was pleasant enough with that square jaw and all his proper manners, but there was something about him she did not like. Something that made her blood chill every time she came in contact with him. Even in the overwhelming heat of the ballroom, she could not seem to keep herself warm in Hurst's presence.

He smiled down at her and she fought the shiver of dread that raced along her flesh.

"I hope you are enjoying yourself tonight."

She forced her lips to curve into a welcoming smile as she offered her hand. He bent over it. Even with her skin protected by gloves, the top of her hand grew cold. Bile rose in her throat as she watched him. Most women—especially women decidedly on the shelf and with no dowry—would kill to be this close to him. The idea that she wanted to flee whenever she spotted him made no sense.

"I always enjoy the Smyth's ball. It is very amusing." She tugged on her hand, twisting it to free it from his grasp. "And you, my lord?"

"I thought to ask for your hand in the next dance." The moment he said it, the first strains of a waltz filled the massive ballroom. A sick ball of dread filled her stomach. "I assume you are free?"

His smirk told Cordelia he knew she did not have one dance on her card. She rarely did. She was not on the marriage mart, far too old and poor to grab attention—except from the Viscount. Now she regretted not securing a dance partner for the first waltz.

"I--"

"Lady Cordelia." A strong masculine voice filled the air around her and sent a rush of heat along her nerve endings. Even without turning she knew who stood behind her. The man she had been chasing for three days straight. The man she was positive ran illegal businesses in London. The subject of her now-due article.

Nicodemus Blackburn.

She turned to face him, her heart beating hard against her breast. As blood rushed out of her head, she felt a bit lightheaded. Where the viscount and his patrician features were attractive in a very English gentry way, Mr. Blackburn was dark and dangerous. If women sighed over the viscount, they fainted when Blackburn gave them his attention. Cordelia wanted to be the exception to that rule...but he was heady indeed.

"Yes, Mr. Blackburn?"

"I believe this is my dance."

132

For a moment, she didn't respond. She couldn't. Her mind simply could not formulate a reply. Blackburn, who rarely danced and had been known for disdaining most of the ton, had just asked her to dance. No. He lied and said she had promised him the dance.

One black eyebrow rose as she said nothing. The curving of his lips was enough to pull her out of her trance.

She offered him her hand and said to Hurst, "If you will excuse me, my lord."

Hurst tossed Blackburn a nasty look before offering her a pleasant smile. "Of course. Perhaps the next waltz?"

She merely smiled but said nothing. Cordelia would make sure not to be in sight of the viscount. Blackburn led her out to the floor and pulled her closer, swinging her into the rhythm of the dance. She drew in a deep breath. The scent of bayrum filled her scenes. That lightheaded feeling returned.

"A bit of advice, my lady."

She looked up at Blackburn trying to keep her wits about her. Everyone sought information on this man, especially her editor who had told her to dig into his character and find out just where he got his money. And he was here, like a ripe peach for the picking. She had a list of questions memorized. Unfortunately, she found herself staring into his mesmerizing eyes and could not gather her wits long enough to ask him anything.

It was Blackburn's fault. His attractiveness did not come from a trained valet who knew how to dress his employer. He possessed the most remarkable gray-blue eyes and blacker than midnight hair—worn unfashionably long. He was put together well, solid. She

133

could feel his muscles flex as he guided her through the waltz, maneuvering around couples with ease.

His attractiveness turned heads, but there was more to it than that. It was the strength she sensed beneath the surface of the polished veneer. Something about him, dangerous and male, seethed just beneath his polite façade. It almost made her giddy to be this close to him.

"Lady Cordelia?"

She blinked. "Yes? Oh, you had advice."

"You should stay away from the Viscount."

She nodded at his comment. No, not truly a comment. A command. She didn't know Blackburn, knew nothing of his family—and he only could know of the gossip surrounding hers. But, for some unknown reason he felt the need to tell her what to do. Of all the cheek!

"Whatever to do you mean?"

His eyes flashed with irritation as they narrowed. "I mean the man is trouble. I fear that he is after but one thing in his pursuit of you."

Where was the tact Blackburn was famous for? Everyone in the ton knew her situation, or thought they knew. It was much worse than she let people know, otherwise she would never be invited to these functions. And while everyone attending knew that her brother was drinking away her inheritance, none of them knew she was so close to living on the street.

People may gossip about her, but they did not do it in front of her. Did Blackburn realize he insulted her? Looking at his serious expression, she thought not. The man actually thought he was helping.

She adopted her most innocent look. "What would that be Mr. Blackburn?"

His expression blanked as he studied her. "I beg your pardon. I was led to believe you were somewhat of a..."

"What, sir?"

Oh, he did not like being put in the corner, but she was happy to shove the man there. The gall of him to insult her so. Granted, she was positive Hurst was after her for the reason Blackburn implied. Though, even that was odd because the viscount could have his choice of most women of the ton—married and unmarried. Why he would want the Lady Fionna's bastard daughter who had no dowry and penchant for books? His pursuit made little sense. But, most men of the ton had little sense.

With an aggravated sigh, he maneuvered them through the French doors out onto the patio. Light from the ballroom spilled out over them as the cool night air hit her skin, cooling her anger and desire.

Blackburn hesitated, then released her. The dark night surrounded them, the tension in the air rising. She walked away from him, to the edge of the terrace. "Whyever are we out here?"

When he did not answer, she turned to face him. He placed a hand on each of his hips and frowned at her. Again. "Stop playing the simpleton."

She blinked. "Playing?"

"Lord Hurst is not a well man."

That was not what she expected to hear. She dropped all pretense. "Not well?"

He hesitated then said, "There have been rumors about him."

"Indeed. There are rumors about almost every eligible man here tonight, including yourself."

He nodded in acknowledgement. "He has certain...tastes that would shock you."

"Do you mean he frequents the House of Rod?"

That had his eyebrows rising. "You know of that?"

"Why do you think I accepted your dance? I didn't have to. After eight years in the ton, I am well aware of how men behave. I know there is something wrong with the viscount."

His gaze sharpened. "You do?"

His intense study suddenly made her very wary. It was if she were a specimen he was trying to decipher. Blackburn's attention filled her with an unusual flash of warmth.

"Y-yes. He...well, he acting just a bit strange." She could not come up with another way to describe it.

"Strange?"

She nodded. "Quite."

He sighed. "Well, thank goodness you have some sense. Most women swoon over him."

"Yes, but as you said, he isn't after my hand in marriage. Many ladies have set their cap for him. *I* am not one of them."

"Indeed. I do apologize for my insensitivity."

She waved it away. "You are not the first, and you will not be the last."

With a smile, he offered her his arm. "If you would allow me to walk you back into the ballroom?"

"Before you do, could you answer one question?"

He dropped his arm as his brow furrowed. "That depends."

"I understand you are in the shipping business."

"Yes."

She bit back an irritated sigh. He was not going to make this an easy task. "There have been some questions about the nature of the shipments."

His expression darkened, his eyes narrowing again as he studied her. As his gaze moved over her face, but

136

she did not allow her own to waver. Breath clogged her throat; her pulse doubled.

"I import many things, Lady Cordelia." She opened her mouth to ask another question, but Blackburn took another step closer. He towered over her, but she did not feel threatened as when other men did it. She felt...hot. Her whole body shimmered with heat.

"My company is known for its fine silks. I understand they are in demand by many ladies. Have you ever felt truly fine silk?"

She could not answer. His voice had dipped lower, caressing her like the fine silk he spoke of. Cordelia knew she should step back, but she could not make her feet move. He inched closer, his legs now brushing the front of her dress.

When she did not answer, Blackburn continued, leaning down to place his hand on the stone wall behind her. He was now much closer than propriety allowed, and her heart threatened to beat from her chest.

"Fine silk slides against flesh," he murmured.

His breath heated her earlobe. Cordelia pulled in a deep breath trying to regain her wits. But her breasts brushed against his chest and tingles shot through her body like shooting stars.

She shook her head. Other questions swirled in her brain, and she knew that Blackburn was trying to divert her attention. Her body did not care. Need coursed through her veins, urging her to move closer, into Blackburn's heat.

At that moment, a group of younger people came out laughing and talking, their excitement of the season easily heard in their voices. Blackburn's head whipped around, and a growl rumbled in his chest. For a moment, she thought he might attack them.

"Mr. Blackburn."

She whispered the words as not to gain the others attention. He hesitated, then looked down her. Fierce hunger darkened his eyes. Cordelia was not sure he even heard her, but a moment later, his expression blanked, the harsh lines of his face smoothing. He drew in a deep breath, then stepped back, the cool night air replacing his heat. She shivered as goose bumps rose over her flesh. Cordelia should be thankful he had pulled back in time. With her background, she had to be careful. There was always a chance that she would step over the line. And at that point, her invitations would stop and she needed them to earn money.

He offered her arm once again. "May I escort you back to the ballroom, Lady Cordelia?" He pitched his voice just loud enough for the group to hear.

She nodded, laying her hand on his arm. "I do thank you sir for your help. Hurst is a nuisance and I could have deflected him. Your help just made it much easier."

He guided her over to a group of matrons. "I trust you will be able to avoid him in the future."

It was not a question, but an order. Odd, because, before tonight, she had barely spoken to him. She sent him a sharp stare to tell them man he had overstepped his bounds. Little shock that he ignored her.

Instead, he bowed and, loud enough for a group of nearby matrons to hear, he said, "Thank you for the dance, Lady Cordelia."

She had been in his company for the last five minutes and had yet to ask him more than one question about his finances. As she stared at him, that eyebrow of his rose again. Mr. Blackburn knew she had questions for him...which was why he had avoided her for days. Now that he was dumping her with the matrons, she had no way of asking them. She was stuck—and he knew it.

She offered him a smile she reserved for the most vapid of young misses. "You are most welcome, Mr. Blackburn."

His lips twitched as if he repressed a smile. After a nod to the matrons—watching the whole scene as if they were at the theater—he turned and walked away.

And Cordelia cursed herself again. She still didn't know if the man earned his money legally or not. She thought back to the dance, the way his body pressed against hers, the heat she saw in his eyes and sighed. She had to learn how to keep her wits about her the next time she encountered Mr. Blackburn.

Her livelihood depended on it.

*

"You look ready to faint, Blackburn," Grayson, Duke of Nothingham said, amusement threading his voice. "Done in by a little mouse of a woman?"

Nico threw him what he hoped was a nasty look and grabbed a drink as a waiter passed by him. Bloody hell, his hand was shaking. "You are treading on thin ice."

"I've never known Lady Cordelia to have this affect on anyone but Hurst, and seriously, I cannot understand why he is interested."

Without knowing or caring what the drink was, Nico tossed back the contents in one huge gulp, wincing as the warm lemonade slid down his throat. God, he needed to get out of there, find a woman. The moment he thought it, he caught sight of Lady Cordelia. His body responded as if he'd been struck by lightning.

"So, tell me, how did Lady Cordelia ensnare you? Was it her modest gown, or her discussion on anything political?"

139

How could he explain it? Not once in society had he come so close to losing control. How could one petite, blue-eyed miss have brought him so close to the edge? Even now he had to grind his teeth together to keep his incisors from descending. He had been moments from taking her, and she would not have resisted. It was in her makeup to respond to him—even if she did not understand. His plan to divert her attention had gone horribly awry. Even now, he could remember the feel of her hardened nipples as they lightly brushed his chest.

Damn! He pulled his attention away from Lady Cordelia and back to Gray who was now studying Nico with enjoyment.

"She's a Carrier."

Gray's face lost all emotion, his body turning to stone. "You must be mistaken. I know every Born in the ton. She is not one."

Nico glanced around looking to see if anyone had overheard and realized that the only attention they had were from eligible young women across the floor. With a sigh, he motioned with his head and turned, not even waiting to see if Gray followed. Nico knew the duke would. He found the library easily, and was relieved to discover it empty. Gray shut the door quietly and leaned against it.

"Do you really think she is a Carrier?"

"I don't think. I know. At age five hundred, I think I know the difference between a Carrier and a normal human female."

"She is not descended from any line I know. Her mother was married to the Earl of Collingsworth."

"He must not have been her birth father."

The look of comprehension slid over Gray's face. "Of course. Only the oldest is his, the son. The daughters were said to have different fathers, all four."

"Yes, and the youngest, Cordelia, is treated as an outcast by the others."

Gray sneered. "That brother of hers is a bastard. Owes everyone in town, which is why he isn't here."

"You mean she is in town alone?"

Gray crossed his arms over his chest and frowned. "Indeed. I think she stays in the family townhouse, but with little staff. Truthfully, I have no idea how she affords it. Her father...Collingsworth left her barely anything to live on from what I heard."

"And there is no rumor of impropriety. She has no protector?"

"Not that I know of. And I assure you, with the notorious Lady Fionna as her mother, if there was a hint of scandal, it would be all over the ton."

Nico shoved that aside and moved back the subject on hand. "Regardless, she is a Carrier."

"Again, I point out that my family has kept track of all the noble families. She isn't on that list and neither is Lady Fionna."

Irritation turned Nico's voice sharp. "Think. When the church attacked us during the Inquisition, many families hid. We scattered to the winds, and I am positive we have yet to find everyone. There are probably several dozen Carriers in the ton and they have no idea...why would they unless they have mated with a Born? "

He had known about Lady Cordelia for days. Something about their first meeting, the way his body had reacted, had told him she was not just a simple bluestocking. He had immediately responded to her, despite the fact she was not his type of woman. He

141

usually liked females tall, lithe and definitely experienced. Cordelia had none of these attributes, but she was a Carrier. So he was predisposed to respond to her.

Though in truth, he had never reacted even to another Carrier so strongly.

"You may be right," Gray surmised.

"I am. It's easy to scent a Carrier. It also explains why Hurst is after her."

The young duke crossed his arms over his chest. "Hurst is not one of us."

"Indeed. He's Made for sure."

With satisfaction, Nico watched Gray's eyes widen in alarm. It was the first Made vampire to hit the ton in recent times. "Bloody hell."

"Precisely. He has shown little to no interest in Lady Cordelia until recently. We need to find out where he was before his fascination arose. If he has not left town..."

He let his words trail off letting Gray draw his own conclusions. "And a nobleman at that. This is not a good development."

"No. I need you to find out where he was, discover any of the places he frequents. Who he's spent time with. We also might want to put a man on him."

"Do you think we need to warn the other noble houses?"

Nico snorted. The other vampire families were notoriously stubborn. "Would it do any good? They refuse to believe there is a problem. My father is the only patriarch who is worried. No one else but the three of us seems to understand the gravity of the situation." He thought about Lady Cordelia and her role in everything. "I say that Hurst's attention started just over a fortnight ago. Something must have happened then. He does not appear to have gone completely into the Blood Lust, but there is a good chance he is not far from sinking there."

"How do you know he isn't already there?"

Sometimes Nico forgot that Gray was too young to have seen Made vampires and their terrible descent into murderous madness. "If he had, you would have seen more than just a slight altercation when I asked Lady Cordelia to dance. It is very likely the bastard would've challenged me on the spot—possibly even attacked me."

Shock crossed Gray's face. "Truly? That would have been a sight."

Nico ground his teeth again, but this time not to keep his teeth hidden. Gray was a good sort, but he was young, especially for a vampire. He was not around for the last purging, and he did not know just how bad this mess would end up.

"He probably doesn't know I am a Born, has no idea what is going on. His body is telling him to pursue her. And since she has no protection, such as your sisters and others in the ton, he knows she would be easier to prey upon."

"I'll get a man on him, and I'll talk to father about his connections, where he has been before. I hope this doesn't end up like that bit of business you had to handle up north."

With that, Gray left Nico alone with his dark thoughts.

There would be no way out of it; Hurst would have to die, but not before they got some information out of the bastard. The one he had to kill three weeks ago had been too far gone to question, but Hurst seemed to still be functioning surprisingly well...but Nico didn't expect that to last. If they could grab the viscount off the street, they might be able to persuade him to talk. He'd make plans tonight with Malik. Time was precious when a vampire had been Made. If they were not handled properly, they would turn into a craven beast searching out the nearest Carrier to consume. If the woman didn't die, she would wish she had.

Now Hurst had apparently set his sights on Lady Cordelia. And that bothered Nico. Exceedingly.

With a sigh, he straightened away from the desk. His body was still humming with anticipation of a joining. While he could not satisfy the mating call Lady Cordelia had nearly wrested from him, he could find a woman to slake his lust.

He walked to the door but it blew open, bringing Lady Cordelia with it. His body responded immediately. The normally perfectly coiffed curls that dangled over her ears were in disarray. A look of irritation marred her usually smooth features. She slammed the door shut behind her and then leaned against it much the same way that Gray had. Clearly, she did not notice him in the room.

"Stupid man." She locked the door behind her and then patted down her hair. "He is becoming a real trial."

"I hope you are not referring to me," Nico said.

She started and then looked in the shadowed corner where he stood.

"Mr. Blackburn?"

He cursed himself the moment he realized she could not see in the darkness. If he had stayed quiet she would not have seen him. She had not mated yet, so she possessed only human abilities.

"It is I. I take from your comments that you did not follow me here."

She sniffed. "Of course not. I am trying to avoid that idiot Hurst. Why on earth he has decided to bother me now is beyond me."

Bloody hell. Hurst's constant pursuit could herald the coming of his blood lust. If the viscount touched her, he'd likely sink into madness. Something would have to be done—tonight.

"Come, now, Lady Cordelia. You could easily attract his lordship's attention for any number of reasons."

She mumbled something under her breath that sounded like "not bloody likely."

At least she understood there was danger. Unfortunately, it did not help his protective instincts. The need to shelter her, keep her safe, coursed through his blood, along with a healthy dose of lust. He did not speak for fear of revealing the depth of his need.

Silence loomed several moments, then without any warning she flashed him a brilliant smile. He blinked as he watched her approach, amazed at the change in her expression. And wary. No woman could be trusted, especially a Carrier. Those with the ability to birth vampires were frighteningly clever—they had to be to survive. He knew without a doubt, Lady Cordelia was working something out in her brain that would only bring about disaster for them both.

"Mr. Blackburn?" She stopped in front of him, her scent wrapping around him, tempting him. It was a mixture of musky woman and innocence that had his incisors threatening to descend. The woman was too bloody tempting for her own good. No wonder Hurst had been after her.

"Yes?" he asked, surprised that he hadn't started panting. Or done something far more aggressive. Even now as she gazed up at him as if she worshipped him. He reacted, his lust in full bloom. He

145

wanted—ached—to throw her across the desk and strip her naked. Nico knew it was primal; it had nothing to do with the woman.

But he'd never had such a strong reaction to a Carrier.

"I wondered..." She pulled her bottom lip through her teeth, and he inwardly groaned. The woman was going to undo him with her innocent gestures. He curled his fingers into the palm of his hands.

"Lady Cordelia, what do you need?"

She blinked and hesitated. He did not blame her. Even he could hear how his voice had deepened, roughened. The earlier altercation still thrummed through his blood. Maybe she would flee the room, and he would be free of her long enough to ease his desires elsewhere.

He should have known better.

She raised her chin, and said, "Can you explain a bit more about your shipping business?"

"W-what?" He could not concentrate on her words, but rather watched the way her lips moved in the slant of moonlight that illuminated her face.

Cordelia cocked her head to the side. "Are you unwell?"

He shook his head, his attention still on her mouth. Her tongue flicked out over the fuller bottom lip as she took a step closer. Bloody hell, he craved to taste her, to feel her mouth move beneath his. He wanted to feel her flesh beneath his and he wanted to sink his teeth into her neck. With every bit of his control, he pulled his mind away from the image of her wearing nothing but the moonlight.

He needed her to go, far away. He made one last attempt.

146

"Lady Cordelia, I think you should leave." He bit out each word, the lust he felt dripping from each syllable. Unfortunately, the woman apparently was oblivious.

She stepped even closer, determination stamped all over her face. Passion darkened her eyes. She was magnificent.

"I will not be deflected again."

Good God, the woman smelled of heaven. He could imagine rolling with her on a bed, the scent of her surrounding him, the tangy taste of her on his tongue. His incisors descended, primed for feeding. He did not even try to stop it. He knew it impossible.

Without another thought, he grabbed her. She gasped, the sound erotic in the darkened library. He had the satisfaction of seeing her eyes widen as he dipped his head.

"Mr. Blackburn, whatever do you think you are doing?"

"Shutting you up."

Then he bent his head and took possession of her mouth.

Enjoy the following excerpts from two independently published authors with series that readers are raving about!

First, from Kris Cook, now available in digital and coming in print as part of The Secret Diaries Vol 1 print anthology, Lea's Ménage Diary:

When Lea's fiancé breaks off their engagement, she is sad but actually more relieved. Life with him would've been nice but boring—especially in bed. But what options are there for her, a single woman, size sixteen, in the dating pool?

Her cousin, Mia, plans a special night out for Lea to get her out of the dumps. The instant they arrive at the BDSM club, she bumps into Kane and Reed, twin brother Masters who are mouth-watering, muscled, male perfection. Shocked at their advances but ready for adventure, Lea jumps at their offer to train her as a sub.

It's much more than the cuffs and ropes that bind her submissive heart to the brothers. Can Kane and Reed prove to Lea that they love her and her curves, or will she refuse to surrender all, holding onto a false body-image that destroys her only chance at love?

Enjoy the following excerpt from *Lea's Ménage Diary:*

Mia leaned into Lex, and I could clearly see the utter joy and happiness on her face. These two were completely in love, not the lukewarm, lackluster fondness I'd felt with Jerry, but the head-over-hells, heart racing, can't-live-without-you, wild and crazy kind of love. My own heart ached for that, but I doubted I could ever feel such a thing with anyone. Hell, I had trouble feeling anything at all. Whenever I did reach into my emotions, they were always muddled and hard to explain. Often, I felt cut off from my own self.

"Shall I show you what I've set up for you, Lea?"

Set up? He must be talking about the tour. I choked out, "Yes. I'm ready. Lead on."

We walked into the reception area.

"Give me a consent form," Lex said to the woman sitting behind the desk. She nodded and pushed over a pen and some papers attached to a clipboard. He wrote on the last page and then handed it to me. "Lea, read this and sign it for me please."

Though he'd said "please," it didn't sound like a request but more of a command. I found his demeanor odd, but somehow comforting. Still, I wondered what kind of place required a person to have to sign release forms. It wasn't like I was going to be bungee jumping tonight. Or was I?

I skimmed the contents, which caused my hands to shake. Along with the legalese of the release, it had some information on what a new client could expect. There were some Dos and Don'ts, and more. Being a single woman here apparently did have its privileges. No one was allowed to approach me without the permission of the Dom acting as my guide in the club. Lex had put his name in that field. Strangely, I felt relieved to sign the thing.

After I signed my name and dated it, I gave it back to Lex.

He looked it over and nodded. "Perfect."

"Where are we going, Master?" Mia asked.

I was shocked to hear her call him that, but in an odd way, it did seem appropriate.

"To one of the training rooms. Reed and Kane are waiting for Lea."

"What?" I squeaked out.

Lex grinned. "Not a what, Lea, but a couple of whos."

I frowned. "*Who* then?"

"You'll be perfectly fine with the twins," Mia chimed in.

My cheeks burned hot. I wasn't ready to meet any new men, but it was clear that Mia had put Lex up to finding me a date. Apparently, I was being given a choice between two. Or was I? Did they mean for me to jump into this hot pool with both feet and into my first ménage?

My old doubts almost shoved aside my timid nature and allowed me to voice my concerns—*almost*.

Lex folded the papers and stuffed them into his jacket, handing the clipboard back to the receptionist. "Let's get on with your tour, little lady." He put his left arm around Mia and his right arm around me.

I walked beside Lex and Mia with my lips pressed firmly together, shaking like a leaf but also so very curious. My emotions, normally buried deep in my psyche, were clear and powerful, jumping with a crosswise mix of cautious anxiety and wicked eagerness.

We went down several hallways and got a glimpse of the "scenes" Mia had informed me about earlier. The very atmosphere of The Cell was thick with sexuality, and its patrons were both beautiful and dangerous looking. I felt totally out of place, and my apprehension grew.

We came to a hallway with only four doors but no windows looking into the rooms. They were marked with the letters "A," "B," "C," and "D." Lex led us to the door with the letter "C" on it.

He knocked, and oddly, I felt a tingle spread through me. I wondered why I was reacting this way.

The door opened, and two of the sexiest men I'd ever seen in my life stood there.

The one with the long, dark hair smiled, causing me to go weak in the knees. "You must be, Lea." He extended his hand for me to take. I did. He squeezed my hand, and a hot jolt shot up my arm from where we touched. "I'm Reed. Welcome."

He wore a tight, black sleeveless T-shirt that accentuated the thick muscles it covered. His biceps bulged and were decorated with gorgeous ink. The left tat was an intricate design that looked tribal to me. The right tat was of a formidable-looking dagger that was softened a bit by the wings it was on top of. His eyes were light brown and surrounded by the thickest lashes I'd ever seen on any man.

"Are you going to hold hands all night or are we going to get started on the training?" His twin asked. Except for his shaved head and different tats, the two Doms were identical.

"S-sorry...I-I'm new to this," I stuttered, jerking my hand back.

"Stop it, Kane. Don't scare the girl away," Reed interjected.

Kane shrugged and then reached out and cupped my chin, causing my belly to flip-flop. "I don't think she'll bolt, bro. I can see excitement in her eyes."

For more info, visit Kriscook.net.

And, from new rising star, Lexi Blake, the second in her bestselling series *Masters and Mercenaries*:

The Men with the Golden Cuffs
Lexi Blake
Copyright 2012 Lexi Blake

Coming May 2012

A woman in danger...

Serena Blake is a bestselling author of erotic fiction. She knows how to write a happy ending but hasn't managed to find one of her own. Divorced and alone, she has no one to turn to when a stalker begins to threaten her life. The cops don't believe her. Her ex-husband thinks she's making the whole story up. She has no one left to turn to except a pair of hired bodyguards. They promise to guard her body, but no one can protect her heart.

Two men in search of love...

Adam Miles and Jacob Dean are halves of a whole. They've spent their entire adult lives searching for the one woman who can handle them both. Adam is the playful, indulgent lover, while Jacob is the possessive, loving Dom. When Serena comes into their lives, Adam is certain that she's the one. But Jacob's past comes back to haunt them all. He is suspicious of Serena's story, and his concerns are driving a wedge between him and Adam. But when the stalker strikes, they will have to come together or lose each other forever...

Enjoy the following excerpt from *The Men with the Golden Cuffs*:

"Now, who is this Master Storm?" The question came out on a low, ungodly sexy growl. "Is he your Dom? What the hell is he doing somewhere else when you're in trouble?"

"He's not my Dom. He's someone I talk to. I needed to do a little research. I met him at a munch and we've been kind of feeling each other out to see if he wouldn't mind training me."

One of the reasons she liked Master Storm was her utter lack of attraction to the man. She wasn't in danger of falling in love with the man. If she were honest with herself, Master Storm was a bit of a puffed up douchebag, but he did know D/s. She was looking for practical knowledge, not a man who made her heart pound in her chest—even when he wasn't sneaking up on her.

"I don't know this man. Where did you meet him? On the Internet?"

"I'm not stupid. I met him at a munch. I found a flyer on a fetish lifestyle site, and it invited interested parties to come to a brunch at a local restaurant. First names only. I met Master Storm about two months ago. We've been talking on the phone about his philosophies."

"Have you been talking about what you need?" He was standing way too close. She wasn't even sure how he'd gotten so close. He was tall, at least six foot three, and he seemed to tower over her. His voice was still deep, but it had lost a bit of command.

"Uhm, we haven't really gotten around to that. He thinks we should talk about his rules first to see if I can follow them."

"Drop him. He's not a Dom. He's a man who likes control but not responsibility. He's testing you to see if you're right for him, but he isn't thinking about what's right for you. That should be his first and only qualification. A Dom should find what he needs, too, but what every good Dom needs is to do right by his submissive. If he hasn't even asked what you need, he's wrong for you." His eyes became hooded, and his gaze slid to the floor as though he didn't really want to look her in the eye. "You should talk to Ian Taggart. He owns Sanctum. He makes it his business to match well-meaning subs with good Doms."

She shook her head. The last thing she needed was to get more into Lara's friend's business. She'd done all right on her own so far. "Thanks, but I can handle it."

Now his eyes came back up, narrowing. "It's obvious to me you can't."

She was a little offended. He barely knew her, but he was making judgments already? "I didn't ask your opinion, Mr. Dean. But I'm curious. It's obvious you can't stand me. I get that a lot. What exactly is it you don't like?"

He crowded her just a bit, almost daring her to back away. Serena felt small and a little helpless against him. "I never said I didn't like you. You're a beautiful woman."

"But you don't seem to like me. You seem to like scaring me." He wasn't scaring her now. Fear wasn't what she felt.

"I did that for your protection. You need to know how vulnerable you really are. You aren't taking this seriously."

He said it quietly, as though he actually cared. It brought down her resentment level. It did nothing to bring down her frustration, but still, as she spoke she found herself doing so in a polite, respectful manner. "I don't understand. I did everything the cops told me to do. I hired a security firm to install an alarm system."

"It's not very good."

"How am I supposed to know that? I don't know anything about this stuff. I paid for it. I know Mojo isn't a good guard dog, but he was so sweet, I couldn't let them

154

put him down. And I have a friend who comes over and walks the house and makes sure there's no one here before I lock myself up for the night."

"It's not enough. Unless there's something you're not telling me."

Humiliation washed over her. She knew what he was saying. "If you don't believe me, you should leave. I'll be fine on my own. I'm obviously just an attention-seeking whore."

He grabbed her elbow. "Don't you call yourself that."

"Why not? It's what you were thinking. It's what the cops think."

He stared at her for the longest time. She stood there, feeling ridiculous. Tears pricked at her eyes for the four hundredth time that day. Why, oh why, couldn't she be tough like Lara and Bridget? They would just spit in this man's eyes and tell him to go to hell, but Serena stood there.

"You're really scared, aren't you? I require the truth."

"Yes, some man threatened to hurt me. It scares me. But I think you scare me, too."

His lips curved up. He wasn't as gorgeous as Adam. There was a starkness to his features that kept him from being beautiful, but when he smiled, his face transformed. "You're a smart girl. You keep on being scared. And when I said you were beautiful, I meant it. You're truly lovely, Serena. The only problem is I know not to trust a beautiful woman. Now be a good girl and get ready for bed. I'm going to sleep in the living room."

He stepped away, leaving her a little breathless—and a whole lot frustrated. She'd finally found a man who thought she was beautiful and naturally he didn't trust her.

For more information, please stop by www.LexiBlake.net.

155

Made in the USA
Lexington, KY
18 February 2013